IF I HADN'T MET YOU

A GRIPPING ROMANTIC MYSTERY

SHALINI RANJAN

Copyright © Shalini Ranjan
All Rights Reserved.

ISBN 978-1-68494-866-6

This book has been published with all efforts taken to make the material error-free after the consent of the author. However, the author and the publisher do not assume and hereby disclaim any liability to any party for any loss, damage, or disruption caused by errors or omissions, whether such errors or omissions result from negligence, accident, or any other cause.

While every effort has been made to avoid any mistake or omission, this publication is being sold on the condition and understanding that neither the author nor the publishers or printers would be liable in any manner to any person by reason of any mistake or omission in this publication or for any action taken or omitted to be taken or advice rendered or accepted on the basis of this work. For any defect in printing or binding the publishers will be liable only to replace the defective copy by another copy of this work then available.

To my husband,

I can truly not imagine my life

Had I not met you...

Contents

Foreword — vii

Acknowledgements — ix

Prologue — xi

1. Chapter 1 — 1
2. Chapter 2 — 8
3. Chapter 3 — 15
4. Chapter 4 — 28
5. Chapter 5 — 38
6. Chapter 6 — 47
7. Chapter 7 — 52
8. Chapter 8 — 60
9. Chapter 9 — 70

Foreword

Some stories can only be told in a certain way. They demand a nuance in their telling, a sense of understanding for the plot and characters that go beyond what's on the page. They don't start or end with the story but make one think of what came before and what's to come after. Needless to say, an author writing such a tale needs to have a clarity of thought, a tunnel vision, of what they envisage for a particular narrative and how they want to guide the readers to that point of crescendo in the story that'll make anyone reading the book stop, reflect, and wonder what led the characters to where they find them to be at.

Shalini Ranjan without a shred of doubt has this tunnel vision and clarity of thought with this book. She lures you into the world of her characters, makes you relate with them by giving them tinges of gray, and then ultimately leaves you awestruck with their fantastical journey and where they eventually end up at.

Being an author and a connoisseur of books, I particularly gravitate towards narratives that have layers to them, something under the ostensible surface which, when scratched, reveals the true texture of a piece. I commend and appreciate any fellow author who juxtaposes different elements in a story to make it a wholesome read without muddling it with redundant subplots and unnecessary exposition. Shalini has managed to do just that and has told a fascinating story of romance and the supernatural peppered with a generous dose of feel-good lighter moments that entertains from its first sentence to its last

If I Hadn't Met you is a compact read. A whirlwind tale told with finesse and care, and now that you have picked the book up, I can assure you that you won't be disappointed when you finish reading it.

- Chitra Padmana, Author of Linger, When You're Gone

Acknowledgements

Taking a story to completion is harder than I thought and more rewarding than I could have ever imagined. None of this would have been possible without my better half, Rajesh Ranjan. He is the one who stood by me and encouraged me to complete this story. From reading early drafts to giving me advice on the cover to keeping the munchkins out of my hair so that I could write. He is as important in getting this book completed as I was. My heartfelt gratitude to him for all this. It is said that 'Behind every successful man, there is a woman'. But I am here to say that the vice versa may also be true as in my case!

I'm eternally grateful to my mother-in-law, Mrs. K. Sushma. They say a girl is blessed with two mothers- one who gives her a life and the other one who gives her a life partner. Thanks to her for being my guiding light during times of distress and struggles. It was her desire to see me succeed in my career as a consultant and as an author, that kept me on the right track. She is the one who taught me discipline, tough love, and traditions. She sustained me in ways that I always knew I needed.

My sincere gratitude to my father-in-law, Mr. P Mandal for his encouraging words all the time. He is a propeller in the true sense of the word!

A special thank you to my brother-in-law, Kunal, and my co-sister Poonam, for always lending an ear to my stories and giving their precious two cents as feedback.

I am indebted to my parents for inculcating the habit of reading in me and for always believing in my worth as an author.

Prologue

IN RANKING THE worst days of her life, this one probably wasn't number one, but it was in the top three. As her husband began to throw one excuse after another, Ambika jolted herself free from her thoughts. Perhaps the worst was yet to be over.

"Why the hell is it so hard for you to understand?" Adarsh Singh Shekhawat yelled at the top of his voice. He was unaware of the fact that a little pair of eyes were watching them, else he would have bothered to close the door to their bedroom, "Nothing is going on between us. She is just a client."

"You think I am blind? You think I don't notice hushed phone calls...?" Ambika started to question with the same intensity, however, she paused to find their son eyeing them from the door. She immediately wiped her tear-stricken face and stepped outside, "Rudra? What are you doing here? Where is your sister?"

"Di is waiting for us outside," the seven-year-old replied happily, showing his hands, "I came to put colors on you both."

"Not now son," Ambika said softly as she watched her husband leave the bedroom from the corner of her eye. She reached out for her regular pills she had started taking recently and swallowed one of them with water.

"What are you taking mummy?"

"I am taking a happy pill. Sometimes grownups become sad and this keeps them happy," she answered as calmly as her strained voice allowed for.

"Can I take one too?" The kid asked inquisitively.

PROLOGUE

"Not at all! This is not for kids." She kissed him gently on his forehead, "You are my brave son Rudra. One day, you are going to grow up into a very handsome man and make me proud."

"Maybe we can give some to dad?" the kid asked, his twinkling eyes refusing to look away from those shining white tablets, "He does not look happy either."

"Maybe we will give him one." She answered playfully, "Now go and call your sister. It is lunchtime already."

"Okay mummy!" With a quick nod, the boy sneaked a few pills in his pocket and ran outside. On his way out, he noticed his father speaking over the phone. He stopped on his track to take out one pill and quickly dropped it in the glass of whiskey that lay untouched on the table.

"Come here Rudra," Anjali caught her brother's hands and pulled him to the orchard, "I think I saw a ghost, down among these trees!"

"Ghost? Where?" he laughed loudly, "You are such a little girl di! Don't worry. Now that I am here, the ghost won't dare hover around anymore."

As both the kids started competing with each other, between playful banters and throwing color-filled water balloons, celebrating the festival of Holi, something sinister was happening inside their home. It had hardly been an hour when they heard a scream from their father. Both of them rushed inside to find their mother lying on the sofa.

"Anju, Rudra, look what's wrong with your mother..." their father spoke hysterically, "she doesn't wake up!"

As the kids looked around nervously, the young boy noticed the glass of whiskey placed right next to her mother, with its content empty.

"Bhaiya, I have called the ambulance," Manohar rushed to his elder brother's side, "Please, take care of yourself.

Bhabhi will be okay."

Destiny sometimes works in mysterious ways. Ambika was declared dead as soon as she reached the hospital. The doctors declared her case suicide by drug overdose.

Soon after they reached home, relatives had come to their house to offer condolences. Their father killed himself with a gun the very same night.

There were two funerals the next day. Overnight, the young siblings had grown up by a decade. While Anjali engaged herself in receiving condolences from relatives, her brother completely closed himself in a shell and refused to speak to anyone.

"I still can't believe my son and my daughter-in-law is dead. Ambika was always smiling, so young and full of life," Gayatri, their paternal grandmother, ruminated over the fate that Ambika was subjected to, "I guess I never realized that she was so sad that she didn't even think about her two children before taking her own life! I hope that she finds her peace, wherever she is!"

The glass of water fell from Rudra's hands and he ran inside. Anjali followed soon after to find him hiding his face in the pillow and crying.

"Rudra, talk to me!" Anjali ran her hand over his head soothingly. She could feel the grief hanging over their heads like an ominous cloud, "It is okay. I am here for you." She whispered, noticing the hesitation in his body language. Something was bothering her little brother and she knew that if not pushed to the edge, he would eventually keep everything bottled up inside him until it ate him alive. She had to keep him away from self-destruction.

It was at that moment when Rudra began to cry. The tears rolled down his cheeks in broken streams and he spoke between sobs, "This is all my fault di. I saw mummy taking those pills. She said it makes her happy," he choked out, his voice so high pitched that Anjali could barely understand him, "So I put that in dad's drink... but then, I think mummy drank it later. I killed her!"

"Shhh. No, you didn't do anything Rudra!" Anjali comforted her little brother, trying to keep the sobs she was holding in, at bay. She was already crying from within and she knew that if her little brother saw that, it would only make the situation worse, "I know you can never do such a thing. So, let's not talk about this ever! Everything will be okay, trust me."

As his sister caressed his hair and rocked him to slumber, sleep was the last thing on his mind. As much as Rudra wanted to tell himself that eventually, all the pain would dissipate and that everything would go back to normal, he couldn't shake this unsettling numb feeling that was penetrating his every sense. He knew nothing would ever be the same now, and on some level, he believed that it was his fault.

Soon after she put her brother to sleep, Anjali walked outside to the lawns. Then she stopped and looked down at the orchard, where she had seen a movement a day before but had dismissed it. Now a gracious black crow was perched on one of the trees. She turned towards the Sheesh Mahal that stood resplendent in the full moonlight. It exuded a warmth that drew her in again. But she resisted the feeling, knowing well that they were leaving the next morning with their Nani. It was time to bid goodbye to the place that had been her home for the last ten years. The happy memories from not so long ago blazed brightly in her mind. With a dull resignation, she closed her eyes and sent a silent prayer for her mother.

~-~

PROLOGUE

Welcoming a new baby into their world is one of the most exciting things for a new parent. But for the Mathur couple, the occasion was more than joyous. They had been blessed with a baby girl after trying for nearly eight years. So, it was only natural that their friends and neighbors had flocked down to their house the next day, soon after the rites at birth were performed.

"Shashiji, have you thought of a name for our daughter?" Garima asked her husband while she gently laid the baby in the crib. The guests had left and the exhaustion from the day was catching up to her. She looked at her husband and spoke fondly, "You know, she goes so easily to anyone who cuddles her. Even during the entire puja of Jatkarma today morning, she hardly ever cried!"

"Garima, we are very fortunate to have been blessed with this girl. See that mole in her left ear? The priest said that this means she will bring good luck, not only to herself but to everyone around her," he spoke proudly, "She is going to bring us all happiness... so I have decided that we will call her Tisha."

CHAPTER ONE

Losing a loved one is sad. To lose two is devastating. While life goes on with every passing season, some people find it hard to move on. And if by any twist of fate, they do appear to have moved on, they will still find a shred of wood to hang on to amidst the waves of life, refusing to let go of the pain and the sufferings they consider themselves subjected to. That is why, eighteen years after his mother's death, Rudra found himself in the ring, every time her memories threaten to devour him. It gave him an outlet to unleash the demons warring within him and lose himself to the moment.

The stage shook, the rowdy audience roared, and the air stood as a jumble of sweat and blood. Money was continuously placed on bets as numbers and names were exchanged back and forth. He stood next in line, waiting. The host was going to announce his name. Rudra stood anxiously, thinking back to the events that had unfolded earlier in the day.

The whole ambiance reeked of incense sticks and camphor. A small urn filled with holy water was kept in front of a large photo frame adorning Ambika Singh Shekhawat's picture.

Their family priest was convinced that the untimely death of his parents, specifically his mother, has proved to be a bad omen for the family. The only way to bring peace- to her soul and the family- was to perform a special ritual. Maha Mrithyunjaya Jaap, as the priest explained, was a sacred practice done to help the soul of a dead family member who had been troubled, angry, or depressed in life.

None of it made any sense to Rudra. He had known his mother to be happy and full of life. The priest's words rung in his ears.

"Day 1 of the Maha Mrithunjaya is successfully performed," the priest had announced and proceeded to instruct the ladies, "Now you can serve this food on a leaf outside the house for the crows."

"Crows?" Rudra had asked, amused, "We should rather offer this food to the beggars."

"Crows are considered as the medium to communicate with the spirits and the humans. They are the only birds that can convey messages from their world to ours. The soul cannot eat the food directly, hence it communicates with the crow and hence this whole ritual." The priest had explained patiently, to which Rudra had simply nodded and left.

Bullshit! He didn't believe in any of it.

"Ladies and gentlemen, welcome to the blood bath bash."

The host blew into his whistle and Rudra looked upfront from his small room, backstage. "My name is Vikrant Khurana, and this is my ring. I make the rules and you place the bet! Tonight, we have a new challenger- Mahabali Singh…"

On cue, a tall man with a strong build entered the room. The crowd whistled and parted to make way for him. Mahabali flexed his muscles and walked in with a confident stride. With a focused expression, he bounced up and down and finally stood at one end waiting for his opponent.

"Rudra, is it really necessary to go today? Why do you beat yourself to it? You didn't kill her," Anjali spoke with worry etched in her voice, the kind only an elder sister can have.

"Are you nervous?" she continued when Rudra did not reply.

He smiled, "No. You look a little nervous, though."

"Maybe," she admitted, *"Your injuries from last fight have not healed yet Rudra. And you don't even consider the fact that you are diabetic!"*

"Di, relax! If it'll make you feel better, tonight I won't let anyone touch me."

"How on earth are you going to manage that?"

He shrugged. "I usually let my opponent get one hit at me, to make it look fair."

"You... what?" Anjali was flabbergasted, *"You let people hit you?"*

"How much fun would it be if I just wipe out someone and they never got a punch in? It's not good for business. No one would bet against me."

"That's a load of bullshit and you know it," she crossed her arms and said sarcastically.

Vikrant brought the mic to his mouth and yelled into it, "Our next fighter doesn't need an introduction; but because he scares the shit outta me, I'll give him one, anyway! Ever since he joined the ring five years back, he has been rumored to be the most lethal player. He is unbeatable and the best that I have seen.

Hold your breath people, I give you: Rudra 'Stone Cold' Shekhawat!"

Cheering ensued, the noise level peaked before quietening down to a dull roar. Everyone waited with bated breath.

~-~

A few kilometers away, a different kind of crowd was cheering on a different kind of occasion. An eighteen-year-old girl was cutting her birthday cake. Dressed up in an ivory-white, halter-necked evening gown, she looked surreal. The color complimented her skin. She matched it with a pendant and two drop earrings.

"Happy birthday Tisha..."

The crowd inside shouted. The ceiling was decked up with pink and red bubbles and the floor was covered by helium balloons. She blew the candles and fed the piece to her best friends who had organized the party for her. After everyone had taken turns to hug and wish the birthday girl, Siddharth aka Sid turned up the volume on the stereo and got the party started.

"Come here," he called her aside and lined up shot glasses along the counter of the bar. Pulling out a bottle of whiskey, he said, "This is the way we do birthdays. You turn eighteen, you have eighteen shots!"

"Oh my God!" she squealed.

"Drink them up, birthday girl!" someone from the crowd urged.

"Alright, here's to you Sid!" she exclaimed, and grabbing the first shot glass, she tipped her head back to empty it in one go.

As she made her way to the dance floor to join her friends, Tisha felt something crackle in the air. Her footsteps felt heavy and a strange sense of foreboding dawned on her, the kind she had gotten used to as a child. Her pulse ramped up. She suddenly felt attuned to even the smallest change around her.

'*It's nothing,*' she told herself, '*I am imagining things.*'

Except, the throbbing in her head was very real. She turned towards Sid, who was busy dancing and had hardly noticed her restlessness, "Did you mix something in my drink?"

"What? Are you crazy?"

"I just feel uneasy. I need to get out of here."

"This is your birthday party Tisha," he insisted.

"I know and I am sorry. But there is somewhere else I need to be right now."

Without giving Sid any chance to protest, she hurried towards the door. She closed it behind her, cutting off her friends' distant protest, and stepped out on the road.

And then she stopped.

All the sensations troubling her rushed through her again- the anxiety, the fear, and the certainty that something terrible was about to happen. Despite the traffic on the road, she strangely felt alone. She caught sight of something moving amidst the branches of a tree.

It was a crow. *Just a crow.*

Dismissing her instincts as silly, she stepped forward. Without any direction in mind, she kept walking until her feet came to a halt in front of a building. It looked secluded except for a soft light and small voices coming from its basement. After a moment of hesitation, she walked further, her steps surprisingly steady as she found her way inside.

The sharp cacophony of a whistle cut through the smoky air. The noise startled her and Tisha looked around for the source of the blast. A man stood on a wooden chair, holding a wad of cash in one hand, the mic in the other. He held a plastic whistle to his lips.

"Ladies and gentlemen, I give you- Rudra 'stone-cold' Shekhawat!"

The volume exploded when Rudra appeared in a doorway across the room. He made his entrance, shirtless, relaxed, and unaffected. He strolled into the center of the ring as if he were showing up to another day at work. The lean muscles stretched under his tattooed skin as he popped his fists against his opponent's knuckles.

The men took a few steps back, and Vikrant sounded the whistle again. Mahabali approached Rudra carefully, with the precision of a professional fighter. His fist flew at Rudra's face with incredible speed, but Rudra dodged and rammed his shoulder into Mahabali at full force.

After a couple of blows, Mahabali took a defensive stance, and Rudra went in attacking mode. Tisha stood on her tiptoes and when she lost her line of sight, she inched forward through the screaming crowd to get a better view. When she finally reached the front, Mahabali had grabbed Rudra with his thick arms and attempted to throw him to the ground.

At that very instant, Rudra looked up and for one second, their eyes met. A shiver of worry coursed through her thinking he was going to get hit, but right when Mahabali leaned down to take a swing at him, Rudra rammed his knee into his face. And before Mahabali could shake off the blow, Rudra had punched him; his fists making contact with his bloodied face over and over. Blood sprayed over Tisha's face and splattered down the front of her gown. Mahabali fell to the ground with a loud thud. The room went completely still for a moment and Tisha watched on, transfixed.

Rudra swung his legs across the boundary and stepped towards Tisha; both looking directly into each other's eyes.

"Hi," his stern expression changed into a hint of a smile at the sight of blood on her face and clothes, "Sorry about that."

Back in the ring, Vikrant threw a scarlet fabric on Mahabali's limp body and the crowd detonated.

"Come on stone-cold," he called Rudra from behind.

Without batting an eyelash, Rudra addressed her again, "Are you hurt?"

Nodding her head in denial, Tisha raised her right hand and caressed the bruise on Rudra's face, from his cheeks to the cut right across his lips. The cut was fresh from the fighting and he winced at the touch.

"I gotta go." He mumbled incoherently and backed away while Tisha stood frozen to her spot. She looked fondly at his diminishing frame amidst the cheering crowd and uttered softly, "Rudra!"

CHAPTER TWO

Turning eighteen is an exciting time for any girl. It is the period when you are prepared to bid goodbye to your teens and everyone starts taking you seriously. But to Tisha, turning eighteen had taken her to an entirely different level. She was far too distanced from any kind of normal excitement... for she was busy nursing a headache and calling in sick from her classes.

It was just past midnight when she had entered her hostel in her blood-soaked birthday gown and with no recollection of where she had been to. Thankfully most of her friends were still away at her birthday party and hence she was able to tiptoe to her room and change into her nightclothes. As she had headed towards her bed, Tisha realized that she was shivering, but not from the cold. The weather was too balmy to catch a fever... or a cold.

Too bad, she mused to herself. Even the weather did not seem to be cooperating with her. She had finally fallen asleep in the wee hours of early morning, swaddling herself in a blanket.

"What's wrong with you? Are you sick?" Siddharth's warm voice sounded in her ear. He had stormed to her room at lunch hour, "Do you want me to take you to the doctor?"

"Stop with the questions Sid!" she squeezed her eyes shut as he drew apart the curtains. The heat of afternoon sunlight flashed inside her room and she stretched out her cold toes, "I don't know what's wrong with me. I think am coming down with something. I certainly have a bad headache since yesterday."

"You don't seem to have a fever," he said, touching her forehead to check for temperature, "Drishti said you slept through the morning? She also heard you talking in your sleep."

"Arrgghh. Why don't the two of you leave me alone," Tisha sat huddled in the blanket and said in a flat tone, hoping Siddharth would take the hint and let her be, "I have taken antibiotics. I need to sleep."

"I am serious Tisha. You never miss classes!" Siddharth held one end of her duvet making it clear that he was not letting it go, "Tell me where did you go yesterday, in the middle of the party?"

"That... I don't remember," her expression suddenly turned grim, "but I felt like someone was following me." She cleverly hid the part of finding blood on her clothes. There was no need to discuss it with others until she had her head sorted out. She also had a distant memory of meeting someone but thinking about it made her uncomfortable. And she had enough headache already.

"Are you sure it is not just a hangover? Maybe I can get you lemonade or something?"

"Later Sid. I have to go visit the temple. Amma thinks that it is bad to not visit the temple on your birthday. For all you know, this is God's way of showing me the right thing to do."

"Yeah right!" He rolled his eyes and picked up his mobile to leave. "I will get going then. Oh, before I forget, I got the pictures from yesterday's party. Thought they would cheer you up." He added, taking out an envelope and handing it to her, "Let's catchup at dinner then. Enjoy your temple visit."

"Sure, I will." Tisha grinned and took out the pictures from the envelope.

There were all sorts of fun pictures. From her entering the party to cutting the cake and trying out the shots, her friends had covered it all. Tisha smiled, for the first time in the day. Friends are a blessing in disguise, and she felt thankful for having Siddharth and Drishti in her life. With a new fervor in her step, she got up to take a quick shower and go visit the temple.

Donning on a yellow-colored salwar suit, she applied kohl in her eyes and pumped her face with powder. Dressed like sunshine, she was about to leave when she heard a small commotion from the balcony. Hastily, she drew apart the curtains to find a huge black crow perched on the window sill.

That's very odd, she stood still wondering if she should shoo it away when the bird started crowing and made attempts to enter her room. With no time to ponder, Tisha immediately picked up the envelope of photos and started scaring the bird, hoping it would leave her in peace. As soon as the bird moved away, she closed the windows and noticed that all the pictures had fallen out of the envelope. Swearing at getting late, she picked up the photos one by one and was going to keep them back into the envelope when her eyes caught something strange in one of the pictures. Her eyes widen at recognition.

It was a grainy quality, but she was sure of it. It was a picture of her dancing with friends near the window. Even though it was late night and the curtains were drawn, she was sure that the shadow cast on the curtains was of the same bird. There was no mistaking the size and shape. Hurriedly, she looked at other pictures. Most of the photos taken near the window displayed the silhouette of a bird sitting on the windowsill. She went very still. Her breathing rushed in and out of her lungs and finally stopped for a long moment. She closed her eyes as a chill ran through her veins.

What does this mean?

Her breathing started again. Her eyes opened, the expression in them was distant. The world around her had changed. With a confident poise, she stepped outside the campus, not even bothering to greet the hostel mates on the way out.

She stood on the road for half an hour. She didn't hear the birds chirping around on the trees, nor did she hear the sirens as an ambulance crossed her. Not once did she shiver.

"Take me to Janakpuri," she got into an auto-rickshaw and addressed the driver.

"Where do you want to go in Janakpuri, madam?"

"Keep driving," the tone of confidence was unmistakable in her voice.

~~~

It was the second day of the mahamritunjaya ritual being performed in Shanti Niwas. The priest had just finished enchanting a set of mantras. The house was filled with fumes of the havan. A message was exchanged between Gayatri Singh Shekhawat and her granddaughter Anjali through eyes glances and the latter got up to call her brother.

"I am preparing for a presentation di," Rudra picked up his mobile in the first ring and spoke in a dull voice, "If this is you calling me home for the ritual, then please stop!"

"Good morning to you too Rudra!" Anjali spoke with an unmistakable enthusiasm in her voice, "I know you are busy. But Nani needs you..." she paused and spoke with just a hint of emotional tone which she knew would work on him, "our family needs you dear brother. Are you really going to stay out of it?"

"I can't help it di. There is a board of directors meeting in an hour and I have got to prepare for it."

"That is just an excuse to get away from home Rudra."

"Why would I want to do that?"

"That's because..." Anjali's voice choked, "Because I think you still blame yourself for our mother's death."

"I will see you at night di."

The line was dead before Anjali could try to persuade her brother. With a disappointed heart, she joined back her family in the hall where the ritual was being performed.

As she stood in front of the Shanti Niwas and listened to the sound of the conch shell being played, she felt uneasy. The fumes of the fire ceremony that came out had an odd effect on her senses and she felt strangely drawn towards the place. Oddly, the huge gate of the bungalow that was usually guarded by two security men was deserted and she was able to walk inside, without being questioned.

But the sense of unease failed to depart.

She saw the food decorated on the wide banana leaf and she felt like it was calling out to her. Her feet walked towards it in automation and she picked up a morsel from the leaf. She was just about to eat it when someone called from behind.

"What are you doing? You are not supposed to be inside. Didn't the guards stop you?" It was a familiar voice and she turned her head. An odd feeling of relief washed over her, but she was alarmed when she saw the old man picking up an odd device and speak into it.

Reluctantly she eyed the food on the banana leaf like she had not eaten for days.

"Don't eat that. I am calling the guards," the old man moved forward and tried to block her way.

"Hari Prakash! Don't stop me." She said in a pained voice. With one hand she pushed the morsel inside her mouth, chewing it to savor its taste.

Suddenly, the world changed around her, and she came to her senses. There was a crow perched right in front of her. Alarmed at her surroundings, Tisha threw the banana leaf down, spilling the remaining bits of food on the white tiles, and took a step back.

"Badi Malkin!" A jolt crossed through the old man's veins and losing his consciousness, he fell to the ground with a thud.

"Dear God!" She muttered and rushed in to get help.

Tisha was not prepared for the scene that greeted her inside. The first thing that caught her attention was the huge photo of Ambika Singh Shekhawat in front of the holy fire. Several candles were lit around it and there was a garland of fresh flowers hung on the frame. Her eyes misted as she looked at the small gathering of people sitting in white clothes. Just then, a gust of wind blew and threatened to blow out the candles.

In the background, she could hear several crows crowing out loudly.

"I am sorry to have interrupted, but I need help." She spoke hastily.

"Look at what you have done!" the priest got up from his seat. He did not look happy, Tisha concluded. The whole surrounding felt like a strange foreboding and she wished to escape from this reality, "This girl's untimely entry has rendered our havan inauspicious. It is not possible now to bring peace to Ambika's soul."

She saw another lady get up from her seat and walk towards her. Scared to her wit's end, Tisha prepared herself for another lashing but instead, the lady in front of her politely asked her about the problem.

"It's my parent's barsi today. We are doing this ritual to bring peace to my mother's soul, which was taken away from us very untimely. How can we help you?"

"Someone has fallen unconscious outside. You might need to take him to the hospital," she spoke in broken words, and fearing for her life, she ran outside; stopping only to catch her breath once she was outside the bungalow.

It was a beautiful day. The weird chill was gone, chased away by the religious fumes and she felt warmer than she had in a long time. If it wasn't for the anxiety that kept gnawing at her, she would have felt great. She decided to enjoy being warm and forget about her worries for the time being.

"Hello Tisha," said a soft voice behind her shoulders.

She looked around and looked astonished at the woman in front of her. She was slightly translucent, strangely two-dimensional. Tisha blinked, then squinted.

She looked at the woman, blinked away, and then looked again. A wave of cold shock pulsed through her like a sledgehammer, thickening her blood, numbing her fingertips.

It was the dead woman from the photo.

CHAPTER THREE

As soon as she recognized the woman from the photo, Tisha acted on her first instinct and she ran. Fortunately, she soon heard the sound of bells chime in and figured out that a temple was nearby.

"Hello Tisha," the faint voice came again, causing her to flinch.

"Excuse me," she leaned towards a woman standing in the queue for performing the puja, "Do you hear any voice?"

"What kind of voice?" The woman looked around puzzled, "Are you okay?"

She gestured apologetically and nodded her head.

Okay, so no one else can hear the dead woman nor can anyone see her. Great! Just what I needed. I am hallucinating. Maybe if I ignore the hallucination, it will go away. She told herself firmly.

"I know you can see me," the woman pointed a white finger at her and she shrunk back in her place.

Tisha instantly shook her head and took out her mobile phone, "No, I can't!"

"And you can hear me too," there was a beat of excitement in her voice, "Look, you don't have to be scared of me. I am not going to harm you."

"Who are you then?" She spoke into her mobile. She took comfort in her words. She braved up a little and shot all the questions that were plaguing her mind, "Why can no one else hear you? How do you know my name?"

"I am Ambika. No one can hear me because…" there was a brief, hectic silence, "I am dead… have been dead for the last eighteen years."

Dead! No. No way!

It was one thing to suspect it. It was completely another thing to hear her confirm it.

Tisha tried but couldn't move. She looked at the translucent projection of the woman in front of her with wide eyes and then she peeked to the deity inside the temple, to the throng of people around the temple, praying, wishing, and doing normal things.

Her mind formed one word- *ghost*.

She swayed with shock and held the nearby railing for support. She stared mutely at Ambika, "I don't want any of this," she mumbled, fear in her voice as well as her body language, "I don't want to see you. Go away."

"Believe me, I tried. I have been lying down for so long. And then just yesterday, I was woken up. And I realized that my Mangalsutra is missing. I cannot rest in peace until I find it. You have to help me."

"Mangalsutra?" Tisha questioned and then bit her tongue, "You mean your wedding chain? Sorry, I don't know what to do. Besides, I have my classes. I have to go."

"You cannot run away from me. I can force you to help me, but it would be easier if you just oblige."

"Are you threatening me?"

"Are you saying you don't want to know where you went yesterday… how you got blood on your clothes?"

"Alright. I see your point," Tisha said drily as an understanding dawned on her, "But I can't believe that you are here for some crummy old chain. Why are you here?"

"Don't you call my Mangalsutra that!" Ambika glared at her

and for an instant, Tisha felt sorry for her. *Gosh, of all the weird things that could happen on my birthday, I had to get stuck in this nightmare*! Tisha thought. In any case, it was not her fault that she lost her wedding chain.

"Alright, I will help you. Where do we search for it? I cannot simply walk inside your house and start questioning your family!" Tisha gestured in the direction of Shanti Niwas.

"That's not my house. I lived in Sheesh Mahal, in Lucknow."

"In that case, I most definitely cannot go to Lucknow. Do you remember the last time you had it?" Tisha asked inquisitively. "Do you remember your whole life?"

"Only parts of it. It seems like a distant memory though," Ambika murmured, almost to herself, "Some parts are distant and hazy. But I remember what I need to remember." Her eyes flashed with an unfathomable expression and suddenly her voice became infectious with energy, "Here is what we are going to do. Right now, you need food and I need a plan to find back my wedding chain. Let's go to a nice eatery, get you some coffee while we will chalk out a plan."

An hour later, they were seated inside the Costa Coffee, the route of which Ambika helped Tisha narrate to the driver.

"By the way, how do you know I love coffee?" Tisha asked as she sipped on her cappuccino, "And you still didn't tell me how you know my name."

"Sometimes I just know things. And I have been watching you, remember?"

Tisha rolled her eyes, "Why do you even want this chain? Was it special?"

For a moment, Ambika fell silent and her eyes became distant again. The only sound was of the coffee machines and a couple talking in hushed tones.

"It was a present from my husband." She said at last, "I got married when I was seventeen. I have worn it my whole life and now it is gone."

"Well, that's nice," Tisha said. "But isn't it possible that..."

"I had it all my life. I wore it all my life." She sounded suddenly agitated. "No matter what else I lost, I kept that. It's the most important thing I ever had. I need it."

She fidgeted with her hands, her face tilted down so all Tisha could see was the corner of her chin and again she felt a pang of sympathy for her. At that exact moment, Ambika yawned and stretched her legs, "This is too boring and dull. I have been dead for too long. I need fun and excitement."

"I thought you need your wedding chain?"

"Later..." she said and disappeared while Tisha simply blinked.

Realizing that Ambika wasn't gonna come back any time soon, Tisha swallowed the remainder of her coffee. She was considering leaving the place when her mobile phone rang. She peered at it to see Siddharth calling her.

"Hi, Sid!"

"Tisha, where are you? I thought you would be coming for the classes after lunch."

"Oh yes. I am already on my way back."

She hastily cut the call and paid the bill when Ambika materialized in front of her. There was a strange light in her eyes and it appeared that she was glowing all over. Tisha pulled out her mobile phone and pretended to talk into it.

"Did you just walk out on me?"

"You were being such a bore. I had to go."

"Great. Now I had to go. It was nice meeting you, umm, Aunt Ambika."

"No wait!" she said in excitement, "You cannot go. You have to help me find my chain. Besides, I just met the most handsome man."

"What do you mean, you met a man? You can't meet a man. You are dead..." Tisha stopped in her tracks, "Oh did you meet another ghost?"

"He is not a ghost," Ambika said irritated, "But he is so handsome. I just saw him talking inside one of those office buildings," she gestured with her hands, "He looks like Dev Anand."

"Who?" she said blankly.

"The film star, of course!"

"Sounds lovely," Tisha said absently as she pushed the door and stepped outside the cafe. "OK. I need to get back to my classes and..."

"I want him," Ambika said and to Tisha's surprise, blocked her way.

"I'm sorry?" She questioned and took out her mobile phone, out of habit.

"The man I just met. I felt it, right here. The connection." She keeps a hand on her heart, "I want to go out with him."

Is she joking? Tisha mused, "You are dead."

"I know, you don't have to keep reminding me," Ambika sounded irritated.

"Look, you are dead, so you can't go on a date with him. It is as simple as that," Tisha said at last, in placatory tones. *What is it about being a ghost that she doesn't understand?*

As she moved forward, Ambika thrust a bare arm across her path and Tisha stopped, taken aback, "Ask him for me?"

'What?"

"Ask him out on a date on my behalf, since I cannot do that. If you go out with him, I will feel like I am going out with him."

"You cannot be serious! You want me to go out on a date with a random man I don't know... so you can have some fun?" Tisha felt like she would burst out laughing, "You are impossible, aunt Ambika!"

"I just want one last little burst of fun with a handsome man while I still have the chance." Ambika's head fell forward and she pouted sadly. "That's all I ask before I disappear from this world." Her voice descended to a whisper. "It's my last desire. My final wish."

"It's not your final wish!" Tisha screamed but started to pretend to talk on the phone when people around her started staring at her. Taking a deep breath, she continued, "You've already told me your final wish! It was to find your Mangalsutra, remember?"

For a moment, Ambika looked stumped for words. "This is my other final wish," she said, at last.

"Look, aunt Ambika." Tisha tried to reason out. "I can't just ask a stranger on a date. You'll have to do without this one. Sorry."

"You're really saying no," she said at last, her voice cracking as though with emotion. "You're really refusing me. One last wish... One tiny request!"

"Stop it!"

"Do you know how long it's been since I've had some fun?" she said with sudden passion. "Do you know how it feels like to be trapped in someplace with no memory of the life that was brutally snatched from me? All those years, in a place with no life, no music, no fun..."

It is not my fault! Tisha wanted to yell but kept quiet nonetheless. There was no running away from this one. She stopped in her tracks. "OK! OK! Whatever! Fine! I'll do it."

"You're an angel!" Ambika's mood instantly flipped to giddy excitement. She whirled around, "I'll show you where he is! Come on!"

Tisha followed her. If she was going to do this, she had to be very quick. Or else she would change her mind.

"Where is he?" She walked inside the massive building and looked around the tiled floor. Everything looked expensive and neat.

"In a room upstairs. Come on!"

"I can't just walk inside. There are electronic checking and I would need to show some ID proof," she paused near the reception. Two girls were standing behind a table of badges. A seminar was going on, "Ahh... Idea! You wait here," she hissed back.

"Hi." she approached the girls briskly. "Sorry, I'm late."

"No problem. They've only just started." One of the girls sat up and started scurrying through her list, while the other started picking up the badges, "And you are ..."

"Abhilasha Tiwari," She answered quickly, grabbing a name badge at random. "Thanks. I'd better get going before they close the door." She said and made a run for the door before anyone could question her. Besides, she was sane enough to not give out her real name to anyone here.

She hurried to the security barriers, flashed her name badge at the guard, and rushed through into a wide corridor before anyone could stop her. There was expensive-looking artwork hung on the walls.

"I have no idea where I am. This building holds about a dozen companies. Where is this guy?" She murmured to Ambika.

"Twentieth floor."

She headed for the elevator, passing professional smiles at all the other people around her. On floor 20, she got out of the lift to find herself in another massive reception area.

A grey-colored plate hung on the wall saying 'Panache'.

"Wow! Panache is a big brand. Do you know they recruit from our college almost every year?" Tisha exclaimed excitedly, "I bet this guy you are talking about is some high profile."

"Come on!" Ambika sauntered ahead of her towards a door with a security panel. Thankfully there were no security men there. Tisha easily walked inside. The place was empty except for a dozen meeting rooms on both sides.

"So, where is he?"

"Hmm." She looked around. "One of these doors along here..." She crossed through some of the doors within seconds and appeared by her side, "I found him! He's in there! He has the most amazing eyes." She said pointing to a solid wooden door labeled Room 'Blueberry'.

"Are you sure?"

"I've just been inside! He's there! Go on! Ask him!" Her hands moved in an animated gesture to push her.

"Wait!" Tisha took a few steps back, trying to think this all through, "I can't just storm inside. I need a plan."

The whole idea had started to appear foolish to her. What was she thinking really, before she agreed to it? Until morning, she was in her cozy room and now here she was... ready to enter a strange guy's office.

She approached the door, trying to ignore the fact that nerves had completely taken over her.

Taking a deep breath, she raised her hand and knocked gently.

"You didn't make any sound!" Ambika exclaimed behind her. "Knock harder! Then just walk in. He's in there! Go on!"

Squeezing her eyes shut, she knocked sharply, twisted the door handle, and took a step inside the room.

Twenty professional people dressed in a suit and blazer were seated around a conference table. Everyone turned to stare at the new entrant. A man at the far end paused in his presentation.

Tisha stared back, frozen. It was not an office. It was a conference room. She was standing in a company she didn't belong to, in a great big meeting she didn't belong to, and everyone seemed to be waiting for her to speak.

"Sorry," she stammered at last. "I don't want to interrupt. Please carry on."

Out of the corner of her eye, she noticed a couple of empty seats. Barely aware of what she was doing, she went to pull out an empty chair and seated herself. The woman next to her pushed along a pad of paper and pen. Too shocked to react, Tisha quietly accepted the stationary. She did a mental jig and looked around.

Nobody had told her to leave! The guy giving the presentation had already resumed his speech and everyone had started to pay attention to him. It was like the past ten minutes hadn't made any difference to them. But Tisha was zapped out. She surreptitiously looked around the table. There were close to twenty people in, out of which twelve were men. Ambika's guy could be one of them! He could be the guy with the spectacles. Or the guy who looked like he was too bored to care. Even the wavy-haired man giving the presentation looked nice. He was talking about some charts and speaking in a nervous voice...

"... and client satisfaction ratings have increased, year-on-year—"

"Stop right there!"

A man standing at the window, whom Tisha hadn't even noticed before, turned around. He was wearing a three-piece suit and his gelled hair was brushed straight back. There was a deep frown between his eyebrows, and he was looking at the wavy-haired guy as though he represented a great personal disappointment to him.

"Client satisfaction ratings aren't what Panache is about."

The man with wavy hair looked perplexed at the interruption and Tisha instantly felt a stab of sympathy for him.

"Of course, Rudra!" he mumbled.

"The focus in this meeting is all wrong," The three-piece suit guy frowned around the table, "I will have to travel to our Lucknow office to bring the team there up to speed. But one thing I would like to clarify, we're not here to perform quick fixes. We are here to innovate..."

The conversation tuned out as Tisha noticed Ambika sliding into the chair next to her. She scribbled '*Which man?*' and pushed her notepad across.

"The one who looks like Dev Anand," Ambika said as though surprised Tisha even had to ask.

For God's sake! How would she know what Dev Anand looked like!

She scribbled again. '*Which one?*'

Silently Tisha looked around. Her bet was on the wavy-haired man. Unless it was the guy sitting right at the front; he looked quite nice. Or maybe that man with the specs?

"Him, of course!" Ambika pointed to the other side of the room.

'The man giving the presentation?' She wrote, just to confirm it.

"No, silly!" Ambika giggled, "Him!" She appeared in front of the man with a frown and gazed at him longingly. "Isn't he adorable?"

"Him?"

Oops. In her shocked state, Tisha spoke out loud. Everyone in the room turned to look at her.

She quickly coughed and muttered 'ahem ahem' to avoid being the center of attention. After a couple of minutes when she was sure that no eyes were on her, she glanced up and looked at the man with the gelled hair.

He looked like one of those men who had a naturally charismatic personality that oozed masculinity and control; it showed in his walk, his voice, every gesture that he made. The height and breadth of him were impressive, but it was his face that caught her eyes... his face was too rugged to be boyish handsome, but it was breathtakingly attractive, nonetheless.

In short, he was impressive, rich, but not her type. But it wasn't she who was going out with him, it was Ambika, she quickly reminded herself.

The discussion was ending, and Tisha needed to act quickly if she was going to do this. This was her only chance. She was sure that he would deny her. After all, he belonged to another class and was much elder to her. But at least, Ambika would be happy that she had done this for her sake, and they could then focus on finding her wedding chain. She looked up to find Ambika gleefully drifting in the air. Gosh, does she understand the predicament she had put her in!

"Before we close our meeting, does anyone has a question?" she heard a deep baritone. In contrast to the fury he had displayed a while ago, he now appeared strangely composed.

"I wanted to ask you if you would go out with me."

"Excuse me?" He looked at her as if she had cracked the joke of the century. Her stomach jittered and did a funny jolt and Tisha realized that she hadn't had anything since morning, except a cup of coffee. First, the ghost and now this man. It was unsettling to look right into his eyes. Maybe there was a full moon or something. That had to be the only rational explanation surely.

"Excuse me?" Rudra raised his hand in front of her face and Tisha snapped back to present, flushing as she realized that she had been staring at him all this while.

"Oh, sorry. So, that's what my question was. Now, I understand that you are a busy man..."

"Leave your number with the receptionist. I would go out with you."

It was Tisha's turn to get shocked. She looked slightly up to find Ambika. She was drifting happily in the air. *Yes...* he said *yes.*

There were murmurs in the conference room.

'This is what you need in today's date.'

'You should just know what you want and go for it.'

'We need such young people in our team.'

'I can't believe Rudra agreed to such a thing.'

Rudra was still looking at her, as though he couldn't believe the words coming out of his mouth.

"Errm. Yeah," she muttered, "That is just perfect. This looks like your card. So, I will call you," she picked up a random visiting card kept on the table and walked towards the door, "It was nice meeting you all. Please continue all the good work that you do."

Outside, the bright sunshine was gone, and the sky had turned cloudy. Rudra watched on as he saw Tisha step outside the building. Heavy raindrops had begun to spatter on the sidewalk. His insides were doing a Zumba: heart-pounding, lungs heaving, stomach clenching. It was something he had never felt before. Too bad that it undoubtedly meant he was losing his mind.

What was this girl doing in his office, in his meeting room? How on earth did she land inside? He didn't say anything to his team, for he didn't want to draw anyone's attention to her.

"Rudra, are we good to wrap up?" he heard his secretary come inside, "You have another meeting with our sales team in half an hour."

"Don't worry." He promised, "I will be ready in five."

Another flash of lightning came, along with a clap of thunder even louder than the last. Rudra could sense a storm brewing. He thought of that unknown girl again and wondered if she had made it safely home. He didn't know what had prompted him to say yes to her. But strangely, he felt determined to know more about her. He turned towards his secretary.

"Sonia, did anyone leave their contact details with you, ten minutes ago?"

"As a matter of fact, it was a girl, Rudra!" Sonia said cheerfully as she opened up her iPad for reference, "Her name is Tisha Mathur and she lives on the campus of the Spencer College."

CHAPTER FOUR

"This place is beautiful," Tisha breathed and look around at the grandeur display. There were in The Fisherman's wharf. It would have cost her a fortune to dine in this place but perhaps not so for the suave-looking young man seated in front of her.

"I am glad you like it," Rudra replied. He was already feeling a little restless.

This was the best table in the restaurant. Rudra was a regular and he had ensured they got his favorite corner table. The restaurant décor was all dark wood with large mirrors and satiny red cushions. It was elegant yet homey. The faint spicy smells of oriental cuisine were the perfect compliment. He had wanted their first date to be nothing short of perfect.

But Tisha did not appear happy. Perhaps she liked the magnificence of the place, but he was beginning to doubt whether she really wanted to be here, with him. It appeared to him, that she had tried every move to walk out of their date, if possible. Hell, she hadn't even remembered that it was *today*! Now and then, she would turn her head and look around awkwardly, as though hoping someone to pop in magically. Since she was the one to ask him out, it was a little frustrating for Rudra to feel unwanted!

He looked at her pointedly. She looked so young and so beautiful. *Perhaps, she wanted him to take her to a discotheque or something that is the rage these days!* Perhaps he would do that the next time. He checked his thoughts just in time, astonished to find himself thinking in that direction. He wasn't even sure if Tisha wanted a next time with him!

~~~

Where was aunt Ambika when she needed her the most!

With this single thought occupying her entire mind-share, Tisha blindly toyed with her food. Ambika had practically refused to leave her side for the past fifteen days. She had spent enough time with her ghost-angel, to the point that Tisha started considering it her mission to find her lost wedding chain. That was why, on Ambika's request, she had gone to the police station to file a missing report. However, it didn't help when the inspector had given her odd looks when she reported that the chain went missing exactly 18 years back… right on the day she was born!

It didn't help right now either that Ambika was nowhere to be seen and she was stuck with a handsome stranger, who was growing increasingly impatient with her silence.

It didn't help when Rudra had arrived at her hostel room unexpectedly two hours ago when she was dressed in her regular clothes. And she had made a complete fool of herself!

It was the third day of the week and their last class had just got canceled. So, an instant plan to go out for a movie and dinner was nothing short of impromptu. Tisha had simply gone to her room to freshen up before leaving with Siddharth and Drishti.

The doorbell rang and hoping it was one of her friends, she opened the door casually.

The six-foot-four, ruggedly handsome male standing on her doorstep was neither Sid nor Drishti!

A bolt of shock coursed through her and then she froze.

"Hi." Rudra shot a pleasant smile. "I hope am not interrupting anything?'

"What?" She gazed at him stupidly. He looked wonderful. White shirt, black jeans, a muscled tower of brooding masculinity. The brown eyes with their thick, short, black lashes flicked to her casual appearance and then back to her stunned face. "I thought you would be ready and expecting me."

"I don't understand."

"It is Wednesday Tisha!" He winked and leaned carelessly across the door and asked, "Aren't you going to invite me in?"

"I just... I texted you that we would meet next Wednesday!"

"You texted last week... so the next Wednesday is today."

"Oh," an understanding dawned on Tisha and Rudra noticed the subtle changes in her expression. Without giving her a chance to back out, he quickly responded, "You are not going to cancel on me now, are you? Remember, you were the one who asked me out."

"I know. You don't have to keep reminding me. Give me ten minutes. I will inform my friends and join you." She had conceded reluctantly.

It was after waiting for nearly another fifteen minutes that Tisha decided to break the silence that had stretched between them. Tisha glanced around for the last time, hoping to catch a glimpse of Ambika, somewhere, in the air. She sighed when she realized that she was all alone in this.

Why would Ambika do this to her! First, convince her to ask a strange man on a date on her behalf and now it looked like she had literally disappeared in thin air. It did not make sense. This wasn't fair. Perhaps something had happened to her? *Do accidents happen to ghosts?*

"Whatever it is," Rudra commented half-seriously, "I don't think it has very long to live."

"Excuse me?" Tisha's gaze snapped to his face and she shook herself out of her thoughts.

"Whatever it is that you have been staring at over my left shoulder for the last ten minutes, I hope it has legs and would run away very quickly."

A brief smile tugged at her lips, "I am sorry. My thoughts drifted."

"That is very normal. I have heard that girls usually find me irresistible." He said gallantly.

He had said it so seriously that if Tisha hadn't been so preoccupied with Ambika's thoughts, she would have laughed.

However, in the next one hour, she learned to laugh again. It didn't require any additional effort on her part because she found that Rudra was rather a pleasant company to be with.

Besides, he was so handsome! His hair was a dark shade of brown, beautifully gelled to fall back in style. He was all rugged angles and sharp planes, from his finely carved nose to his chiseled jaw and long fingers. He looked stern and pleasant at the same time.

She came to know that he had started working in his uncle's company and was recently promoted to the position of assistant vice president.

"Hello!" she glanced in front of her to find Rudra snapping his fingers to catch her attention, "have you been following me Tisha?"

"Huh?" she asked, wondering if he could mind read her. She didn't want him to know that she fancied him, a little too much. Besides, he was still a stranger!

A very handsome stranger, nonetheless, she grinned at herself.

"I asked if you had been following me. First, you accost me in the ring and then you almost sabotage my conference," he added flirtatiously, "Is this something you do regularly or am I special?"

"You flatter yourself a little too much, don't you?" she replied with mild amusement, "Tell me something- if my asking you out hurt your male ego so much, why you agreed... you barely took 5 seconds to say yes!"

"Now we are talking!" he paused, as if he was contemplating his next words, "You see, in office, I maintain certain professionalism. You know, being the youngest VP in the system, it is hard for a lot of employees to accept my authority. Dare I say that I tend to carry it even when I am not working? So that makes me a little unapproachable by girls. You were the first girl to ever ask me out so boldly that and that too in my conference room. I was smitten!"

Tisha reflected on the irony of the situation while Rudra continued, "You know that was not the first time we met. You were there the other day too, in the ring! I remember it clearly. What were you doing there?"

"You were one of the wrestlers?" Shocked, she stared at him.

"Yes, I was. You were standing in the front row. You were so close to the ring that your dress got spoiled..." Rudra studied her intently, his face alighted with curiosity, caution, and the dawning of understanding, "You don't remember any of it, do you Tisha?"

She flinched under his poignant gaze and contemplated the option of telling him blunt truth. First, he was a stranger, and secondly, he might find the whole seeing-the-ghost-and-asking-him-out story so ridiculous that he would simply laugh it out. And even if he thinks she is mad, she could maybe live with it. It wasn't like he was going to see her again or anything!

"Can I confide something in you?"

"By all means go ahead," Rudra said, flashing her an encouraging look.

"You know last week, it was my birthday. I had turned eighteen. As soon as I had cut the cake, I had this weird feeling that something was watching me," she paused and felt wretched at reliving the memory again, "So anyway, I excused myself from my friends and stepped out for some fresh air. I might have entered your ring then, because the next thing I knew, I was back in my hostel. My birthday dress was spewed with fresh blood. I was so terrified. I couldn't even call any of my friends. How would I have explained my state to them? No one would have understood." Fresh tears had begun to gather in her eyes and she blinked them back hastily. "The next day, I entered someone's house, saw the lady's photo whose death rites were being performed. When I went to the temple, I saw the ghost of the same dead lady."

"You think I am concocting this whole thing up, don't you?"

"No, I think that..." he said with a barely suppressed smile, "you had a massive hangover. Come on now, let me drop you at your hostel."

"I can manage!" she pushed her chair back and got up angrily, "if you didn't believe what I said, you could have said so without making fun of me. And for your information, I barely had a few shots."

"Tisha, wait!" He quickly paid the bill and pushed back his chair. Because she still looked so forlorn, he put a comforting arm around her and pulled her closer, "I believe you, okay? I just don't want to scare you further by talking about it. Do you understand what I am trying to say?"

He stood so close to her, just next to their table, staring down at her with narrowed dark eyes. She slanted her face away to give herself breathing space. He was physically too imposing, so tall and so handsome. She would have to go on tiptoe to kiss even the hollow of his throat. The aberrant thought shocked her, shook her, and instinctively she guarded her expressions. Realizing that he was expecting an answer, she nodded mutely because she was too lost for words to frame a sentence. Rudra led the way out towards his car. He put his hand on her back as he leaned forward to open the car door. The contact was so sudden and so pleasurable that she almost stumbled. Recovering, she slid on the passenger seat while Rudra took charge of driving to her hostel. They covered the ride in companionable silence with the radio being the only one making the conversation.

"Would you to like come in for coffee or something?" she asked, suddenly wishing she should not have. He was, by far, still a stranger, even though she had confided in him.

"I thought you wouldn't ask," Rudra answered, disembarking from his car. He was smiling again, Tisha noticed. She wished he would stop. It was too distracting.

As Rudra followed Tisha inside, he thought of how gorgeous she was. At the same time, she managed to be an alluringly beautiful woman and a bewitchingly innocent girl. She was a study of intriguing and beguiling contrasts. She had greeted him with a natural warmth that was irresistible and had laughed out loud at his lame jokes. She was refreshingly frank and unselfconscious, yet she was sweet and soft too, enough to have been crushed when she felt that he was making fun of her. In the course of one evening, she had first treated him indifferently and had taken his advances with a stride. And to top it all off, she claimed to see ghosts! God, did she really think she could scare him off or what!

He walked towards the window where Tisha was setting up the electric kettle. He stood at a little distance from her and looked at her keenly. Her face donned an affectionate smile. Her lips were red and lush and appeared as soft as rose petals. Her skin was perfect, with a porcelain texture that would show the imprint of a touch, a kiss. Standing this close to her, he could smell the sweet scent of her skin, and it was so enticing that it became difficult for him to think of anything else.

He knew he shouldn't do it, even as he reached for her. The last thing he wanted was to have a relationship with a girl so young, so innocent. There were perhaps a hundred other reasons too, but at this moment, none of them mattered. His hands closed on her waist, and the feel of her- warm and soft, so vibrant that his palms tickled where he touched her- went to his head like a potent wine. He saw her eyes widen in surprise. Her hands lifted and flattened against his chest, and a shiver of response rippled his skin. Inexorably, his gaze fastened on her lips, he drew her closer until her slim body rested against him. He felt her legs tangle with his, saw those red lips part as she drew in a startled breath. Then he lifted her on tiptoe and bent his head and fed that particular desire.

Her lips felt like rose petals, too, soft and velvety. He slanted his head and increased the pressure of his mouth, forcing them to open, a flower blooming at his command. Blood thundered through his veins and he pulled her tighter, sliding his arms around her and held her closer. He felt her shudder, felt the convulsive movement of her hips, arching into him, and fierce male triumph flooded him. Her arms slid upward over his shoulders, to twine around his neck, and her teeth parted to allow him deeper access. A low growl sounded deep in his throat, and he deepened the kiss. Her taste was sweet and hot, flavored with the strong coffee she had drunk with her dessert. He drove her backward, forcing her against the door. She was a live fire in his arms, not struggling against his kiss, not just accepting it, but responding wildly to his touch. Her lips trembled and clung and caressed. He wanted more, wanted everything.

The electric kettle beeped, signaling that the coffee was ready.

Whether it was the sound of the beep or his reaction to it that broke the spell on Tisha, she suddenly stiffened in his arms and began shoving against him. Rudra caught a glimpse of her tensed face and quickly set her on her feet, he released her and stepped back before she could start accusing him of seducing her.

Instead, she whispered, "No."

Desire skimmed through his veins and frustration started rearing its head. He was sweating, shaking with the need to have her. Yet the desire to comfort her was stronger. His brain won and he put out an arm each, on the walls, effectively restraining her in place, "Tisha, let me explain."

"Please, no!" She said again, "You have to understand. I never do such kind of things."

"I don't do such kind of things either if that's what you mean." Slowly he moved and held her hand so that his fingers meshed with hers. "It is alright. We didn't do anything wrong."

She gripped his hand tightly, completely uncertain of what to say, at the moment. After a minute, he said in a quiet voice, "Will you be okay on your own, if I leave now?"

"Yes," she spoke hurriedly, "My roommate must be on her way, you know. We have assignments to work on and projects to finish."

"All right." He looked down at her and lifted his hand as if to smooth her hair, but then let it fall back to his side. He couldn't safely allow himself to touch her just yet. "I will see you soon. Take care Tisha."

To Tisha, it felt like a promise and she found herself foolishly thinking of Rudra even as she went through her regular assignments and discussions. Her first date with Rudra had been beyond her wildest dreams. So lost was she in her romanticized ideas that she nearly forgot the very person, alive or dead, who had brought him to her.

CHAPTER FIVE

"Try this sandwich." Siddharth pushed the plate in front of Tisha and grumbled, "You are hardly eating anything Tisha. And you have barely spoken to me since we came to the canteen! What is so interesting in your mobile, if I may ask?"

"Sorry, so sorry Sid!" She graciously picked up a large piece of bread and munched it, "I was texting Rudra. I am meeting him today evening."

"Yes, I know. I have heard this at least fifty times in the past one and a half months."

"Oh come on. You don't have to look so pensive now. Did I ever complain when you had started dating Drishti and you barely noticed anyone except her?"

"That was because I was falling in love with her," his eyes twinkled as an idea started taking shape in his mind, "Is *that* what is happening here?"

"Is *what* happening here?" she asked absentmindedly.

"You are falling in love with Rudra!" Siddharth commented tongue in cheek, "That would explain why you are so lost in your phone and why you smile at yourself!"

"I don't know. Isn't it too short a time to fall in love?"

"I can't believe this," he rolled his eyes at Tisha's question, "Tell me about this guy. I have to meet him once."

"There is nothing much to tell Sid." Tisha said dreamily, "Rudra is a simple no-nonsense kind of person. He lost his parents when he was just seven years old. His uncle and aunt brought him and his sister up like their own children. They loved him so much that they didn't even have their child. Rudra works in his uncle's company. And he is as crazy about me as I am about him!"

"Wow. So, what's the big plan for today? You guys going somewhere special?"

"No. Rudra has invited me home for the first time." She said shyly, "Perhaps we will go for a movie from there."

"Are you kidding me Tisha? When a guy invites his girlfriend home, a movie is the last thing on his mind!" he looked at Tisha and continued when she still looked confused, "I think Rudra wants you to meet his family!"

"Ohh. Are you sure? He just said that he wants us to spend some time alone."

"I would say why to take a risk," Siddharth shrugged nonchalantly, "I mean if things are getting serious between you both, meeting the family seems like the next logical step before he could propose to you."

"Ohh dear God, what makes you think he is going to propose! What am I going to wear?" she panicked, "I also need to hit the parlor and there are barely four hours left!"

"Why fear when Drishti is there. She would perhaps lay out a dozen choices in front of you," Siddharth raised his glass in a mock toast and added with a wink, "To Rudra Singh Shekhawat and from wherever did you find him!"

The innocent remark from Siddharth didn't bode well with Tisha and momentarily forgetting her newfound happiness, she started wondering where aunt Ambika was. It had been close to two months since her first date with Rudra. While things had been going too smooth between them, she couldn't help but feel guilty and worried about falling for her pick of a handsome man.

~~~

"I feel like a guest in my own house," Rudra remarked ironically to his aunt as they were taking Tisha on a guided tour of Shanti Niwas. He had not been alone with her since she had come in and that had been more than an hour ago.

"Rudra!" Renuka admonished him gently, "Why don't you go check if Anjali has come already, while I will show my room to Tisha?"

"Come, sit here Tisha." She said after they were alone in her bedroom, "What do you think about my son?"

"I think he is a very nice man," Tisha replied with as much graciousness as she can.

"And?" Renuka prodded her further, "Do you like him?"

She shied at the bluntness of the question and gently nodded her head. Renuka felt extremely pleased, "You know I have brought Rudra up like my own son. It is the least I could have done after he lost his parents at a very young age."

"Yes, Rudra told me about it."

"He told you about it. Well, Rudra rarely talks about that fateful night with either of us. He had barely let any of us visit Sheesh Mahal, which was where they all lived until then. We thought he would never be able to come out of his grief. But I am glad he was able to build a good life for himself..." Renukaka said in automation as if reliving a distant memory and Tisha didn't intervene, "Lovely lady his mother was, so full of life! Perhaps she was not as happy as we thought she was... or she would never have thought of taking her own life!" Renuka checked herself just in time to realize that she had divulged more than what was required. Swallowing a lump, she tried to change the subject, "so anyway, Rudra tells me you study at Spencer College. What do you plan to do after your graduation?"

For a moment, Tisha simply stared at her in shocked incomprehension.

Rudra's mother committed suicide! But he had told her that it was an accident! Did he not know or did he deliberately lie to her about it!

"Aunty!" she spoke softly, suddenly wanting to know more, "If you don't mind, can you tell me how his mother died?"

"Rudra might not like me tell you this Tisha," she said in hushed tones, "but since you asked, his mother suspected her husband of having an affair and she committed suicide by taking a lot of pills. Her husband couldn't take the grief of his wife's death and he shot himself too on the same day!"

"But there was no affair, right? Or else uncle would not shoot himself out of guilt or whatever," Tisha countered, finding the whole idea ridiculous, "And if his mother was so spirited, why would she take her own life instead of confronting her husband squarely... especially when she knew her kids would be all alone without her?"

"We should go downstairs Tisha... and in my son's interest, it would be best if you never speak of his mother again," she said in a clipped voice. Just then, Rudra had arrived, and looking at his cheerful eagerness, Tisha momentarily forgot about all her earlier wariness surrounding his mother's ill-timed death.

"Renu aunty! Di is still on her way. Are you done with your ladies' talk?"

"Not really! You know, Tisha told me about her industrial project," She pointed out, enjoying his discomfiture and his healthy eagerness to be alone with his girlfriend, "Since Anjali's husband has gone to the US and he is not supposed to return a least until a month... Tisha could always move into her house. We could spend some time with her and then you could stay there too... if you want!"

"That idea is as absurd as..." Rudra started to complain when he noticed Tisha's giggling and realized the irony of her aunt's statement. Moodily, he checked himself in time, "That's very helpful aunty. Anyway, I am leaving for Lucknow in a few days. You can spend all the time with Tisha during those days."

"And now we have come to the end of this tour," Renuka walked both of them out towards the other end of their house and said in mock commentary style to Tisha, "As you might have guessed, this one is Rudra's bedroom. Tisha, why don't you go freshen up and I would get some snacks and coffee for you."

Excitement buzzed through Tisha when Rudra turned around and closed the door to his bedroom behind his aunt's back.

Was this the moment when Rudra would propose to her! She started to wonder about Sid's comments and anxiously walked over to the farthest end. Placing her elbows on the window sill, she leaned her frame, wondering how her life had changed in the last two months. *Of course, she loved him*, she decided that the reason her heart starts beating every time Rudra came within her proximity could be nothing else. And she was sure that Rudra had to like her a wee bit for having met her almost every alternate day and taking her out to movies and restaurants.

"Found something you like?"

Tisha swung around, looking startled and pleased and dubious. She didn't realize when he had walked so closely to her. For a moment, she felt herself drown under the spell of his brown eyes. His hands tightened on her, drawing her closer. She held her breath, excited and alarmed at the realization that finally, he was going to say those three words. She needed a diversion from her thoughts. "Your room has the best view!"

"Found anything else you like?"

You, Tisha thought of how close they have come in such a short time. And now Rudra had invited her to his home to introduce her to his family.

"Do you think your family liked me?"

"Is that why you are wearing an Indian suit? So that you can impress my family?"

"Manohar uncle is very gentle. Even your grandmother looks very kind," Tisha continued her monologue, pretending to not have heard him, "But Renu aunt kinda scared me. I wish your sister were here though!"

"I like you enough. Whose opinion do you care about now?"

"Well, when you put it that way..." Tisha raised her head, only to have her words smothered by his lips.

Rudra saw the soft invitation in her eyes. Tipping her chin up, he touched his lips to hers and felt the gasp of her indrawn breath at the same time her body seemed to tense. Puzzled by her rather extreme reaction, he lifted his head and waited for what seemed a long time for her to open her eyes. When her long lashes finally fluttered up, she looked confused and expectant and... even a little disappointed.

"Is something wrong Tisha?" he asked cautiously while he wondered if he was rushing things with her.

"No, not at all," she replied, but it seemed as if the opposite were true.

Rudra looked at her in waiting silence, a business tactic that he had found to be naturally prompting the other person to continue speaking. After a moment, Tisha explained, "It is only that I was expecting something else."

"What was it that you expected?"

She shook her head, her smooth brow furrowed, her eyes never leaving him, "I don't know."

"Perhaps you were expecting..." he said softly as he slid his arms around her waist and touched his lips to her ear, "something more like this."

His warm breath in her ear sent shivers up Tisha's spine and she turned her face away from the cause, which brought her lips into instant contact with his. Rudra had intended to give her a short speck but when her soft lips parted on a shaky breath, all his intentions slipped from his mind.

"Stop!" he heard a faint protest from beneath him, "We need to think through this."

"It is damn hard to think when you are in my arms," Rudra reluctantly loosened his grip on her. With a mixture of disbelief and amusement, he gazed at the exquisite young beauty in front of him. Her face was flushed, her chest was heaving gently with each apprehensive breath she took and her eyes were wide with confusion and desire.

Gosh, everything was so hard when it came to Tisha.

"I think it's time we did something else," he held her hand and moved towards the door.

"What do you have in mind?" she asked shakily and followed him anyway.

"What I have in mind," he said drily, "And what we are going do are two different things Tisha. Let's go down. Nani has arranged for a small Pooja to welcome you."

~~~

"Welcome to our home Tisha!"

Tisha watched on emotionally as the eldest lady of the Shekhawat family applied tilak on her head, warmly welcoming her into her home as well as her heart.

An entire area in the corner of the main hall was dedicated for daily prayers in Shanti Niwas. It was perhaps as big as her hostel room, Tisha noted with awe. On a beautifully designed edifice, idols of deity were kept. An incense burner, a plate full of flowers and fruits were kept in front of the idols. It was only then that she noticed a picture of a beautiful young lady, on the extreme right side of the idols. It was a smiling picture that was adorned with a garland of yellow flowers. Tisha could never forget the face. It was etched deeply in her memory. It was the face because of which she was standing here today.

In a daze of guilt and shock, she bit down hard on her trembling lower lip while her mind seemed to connect the dots. She stood there in frozen numbness... when all she longed to do was run away from here... before she choked on the tears that were suddenly threatening to spill from her eyes.

Gayatri Singh Shekhawat followed her gaze and broke the silence that loomed between them, "She is Rudra's mother, my daughter... who was rudely taken away from us before time." Tisha turned her head in shock from Rudra to his grandmother. Then she looked at Rudra again and demanded, "Aunt Ambika is your mother?"

"What do you mean- aunt Ambika? Tisha, did you know my daughter?" The old lady asked.

Tisha paled like a ghost at the question. She was still coming to terms with the truth she had just discovered. Time and again, her mind flew back to meeting Ambika just after her eighteenth birthday. She thought of how Ambika had told her that she met a handsome man and how she pestered her to ask Rudra out. A part of her understood and a part of her became inquisitive.

"Rudra had mentioned to me about her a couple of times," she said in a calm tone that she was not feeling from within. Suddenly, the room started to feel claustrophobic and she longed for fresh air. Turning towards Rudra, she said, "Can you drop me at my hostel? I remembered a certain assignment I am supposed to submit tonight."

Rudra quickly smothered a frown at her sudden demeanor, "Sure, come with me."

It was only after she was seated within the confines of Rudra's car and they were en route to her hostel that Tisha weighed her next words, "There is something you must know."

"What is it sweetheart," he halted the car and cupped her face to comfort her, "You look pale ever since you met my Nani."

"I think aunt Ambika, your mother, was murdered," she said in a single breath, for she was too scared of her own emotions, "And I think she tried to reach out to me for something."

CHAPTER SIX

The weather in Lucknow was a strange combination of balmy and humid, but Tisha didn't feel any bit of it. Thanks to the AC in the rental car, she thought as she surveyed the route on her phone through the GPS. Sheesh Mahal was barely an hour away now. She had arrived in Lucknow just a week ago for her industrial project and today was her last day here. *And perhaps her last opportunity to find the whereabouts of Ambika too,* she thought. No one apart from Drishti was aware of her side of the story that she indeed saw a ghost, a good-natured ghost... and that she wanted to help her look for her wedding chain. As the traffic signals changed to red, she stopped the car. She couldn't help thinking about her last conversation with Rudra.

"I think aunt Ambika, your mother, was murdered," she had said in a single breath, for she was too scared of her own emotions, "And I think she tried to reach out to me for something."

When Rudra simply looked back at her, she mistook his silence for encouragement and continued, "Remember, I told you about seeing a ghost on my birthday? It was your mother. In fact, it was she who pushed me to ask you out at the conference."

She looked at him pleadingly, "You have to believe me. Please say something!"

"What do you expect me to say to this bullshit?" he said calmly, *"Mom met you. She told you to ask me out. She then followed you around for a month, telling you all about her life. And then she told you that she was murdered?"*

"She didn't tell me how she died. I just concluded it based on what I heard about her today, in your house."

"Spare me Tisha."

"You have to believe me! How else would I be here?"

"Because you have gone crazy!" He slammed his hand so hard on the steering wheel, that Tisha thought it might crack, "I don't know what idea you have formed in your head... but this nonsense needs to stop. You got to stop talking about my mother."

"This... this nonsense?" Heart hammering in her chest, she asked feebly, "You think I am lying about all of it? Then all that is between us... our feelings..."

"If it was my mother who drove you to me," Rudra could barely control his anger. He spoke with gritted teeth, *"...then that makes everything between us a lie too, doesn't it?"*

She had immediately asked him to stop the car and got down. Next, she had called a cab to reach her hostel. Her self-respect had her from breaking down until she reached her room. She broke down soon after, crying her heart for the man she thought she was falling in love with.

But now no more. She was more worried about finding aunt Ambika. Through her research on the internet, she had come across an article that said that some people, who have unfulfilled desires, are not able to let go even after their deaths. The soul of such people tends to linger around, preferably around their choice of people or the place where they had lived most of their life.

So, after assuring Drishti that she was not going to get herself killed and after asking her to be on the lookout in case something happened to her, Tisha had set out on her chanced journey.

It had to be the Sheesh Mahal, of course, Tisha thought with resignation, as she stopped the car at a distance from the huge mansion. Three guards had secured the gate and there were probably even more inside. Even from far, something was alluring about Sheesh Mahal. Ambika had already filled her in with numerous tales of this place. She was sure she could recognize the various lanes and corners. *Maybe, she could also imagine little Rudra running about and playing in the vast lush garden that Ambika had told her about.* Thoughts of Rudra made her wince. She was glad that his car wasn't parked there. It would have been too ironic for him to appear in front of her. Thank God his business required him in Delhi now and that he didn't have the luxury of lazing around in this place. Her stomach growled and she realized that it was nearly dinnertime. Not wanting to delay dinner, Tisha walked on her heels sideways along the boundary and stopped in a secluded stop right in front of the lake.

The earthly scents washed over her, fresh and powerful with spring, and she felt invigorated. Her eyes closed so she could concentrate. There was the rich brown scent of the earth, the fresh verdant of leaves, and the spicy golden scent of pine sap. She inhaled that last with a little shiver of recognition. Rudra's scent contained a hint of that golden spice.

Her eyes popped open. The shivering of her body told her where that fantasy had been going and she reprimanded herself. Walking carefully around the lake for another twenty minutes, Tisha came in front of a porch that led to a small back door. The boards of the porch creaked beneath her feet, but she was far too excited at her discovery of the door that led to the inside. Praying to the almighty that it wasn't locked and there weren't any guards inside, she twisted the door handle.

It opened easily and Tisha walked inside on tiptoe. Fortunately, the place appeared deserted. Everything was clean, though a film of dust was gathered on the surface. As she wandered from one room to another, she noticed a distinct familiarity between them. Each room boasted of a king-size double bed and several artifacts. She could only imagine them because most of the objects were covered with a plain white cloth. She opened all the cabinet doors and drawers, but they were all empty.

Tisha felt disheartened. She had assumed that she would be able to figure out Ambika's room. She had even called her name out loud in the hope that it would register, and she would somehow come back to her. But now, after wandering through nearly a dozen rooms, she didn't feel quite confident.

There was still one last room to check, though she didn't expect to find anything. She had come here on a hunch, an intuition that perhaps there would be at least one evidence that Ambika was really murdered or maybe she could stumble upon the wedding chain that she was so desperately looking for. But so far, lady luck had not been on her side.

The doors to the room creaked when Tisha opened them, but it didn't bother her. It wasn't as if there was going to be anyone here either. Unlike the other rooms, no white sheets were covering the objects here. The bed also appeared to have fresh sheets. The pillows lied about in a disorganized fashion. Momentarily, Tisha considered if someone was living here. But in her haste, she did not pay heed to any of it. After surveying the room, she turned towards the cabinets and the drawers, when there was a sound in the bathroom.

It meant that someone else was there!

Tisha stiffened, her eyes widening with dread as she slowly turned. Like a felon approaching the gallows, her gaze traveled across the tiles on the floor towards the door and then up the door that had just been opened.

Right in front of her stood a very shirtless Rudra Singh Shekhawat in nothing but a pair of boxers, holding a towel in his hands and watching her with narrowed dark eyes.

CHAPTER SEVEN

"I met Tisha today," Anjali said as she handled Rudra his cup of black coffee. She continued sarcastically when he showed no response, "You know that beautiful and attractive girl... who you introduced to Nani as your girlfriend?"

Rudra glanced up, wry awareness in his eyes as he caught the mirth in his sister's expressions, "I know who Tisha is di. Where did you meet her?"

"Here. She came home earlier before lunch. She was asking about mom."

Rudra almost choked. He set his coffee down with a force that made the liquid slosh dangerously close to the rim. "She did what? What in the hell did she want to know about mom?" The thought of Tisha asking anything about his mother made him bitterly angry.

"General stuff. You would be surprised to know the kind of stuff she claims to know about mom. We talked about what mother was like when she was younger, how she met dad... and how she died," Anjali spoke as if recounting a distant memory, "She wanted to know if there was any kind of tension between our parents in their last few days... and if dad was seeing anyone."

"Damn it, di!" Furious, Rudra half rose from his chair, intending to go to her hostel right now and have it out with her.

Anjali stopped him with a hand on his arm. "I felt like mom was also there... with us... just for a moment," she said mildly, "You know, it was Tisha who had come to Shanti Niwas and interfered with our ritual. She had even addressed Hari Prakash by his name. Though, soon after, she had run out, scared."

"That girl is going crazy di." Rudra snapped. "I am leaving for Lucknow today. I will talk to her after I am back. But I'll be goddamned if she contacts anyone of us regarding mom!"

And now, seeing Tisha in his bedroom, in front of her, in flesh and blood, was beyond his wildest dreams. For an instant, they stared at each other across the small distance separating them.

Tisha's thoughts darted about in panic, trying to think of a good reason for her presence, but her normally nimble mind was blank with shock. She had thought herself alone, and then to turn and see Rudra, of all people – a shirtless Rudra, at that. *It wasn't fair!* She needed all her wits about her when dealing with him; she couldn't afford to be distracted by that bare expanse of chest.

Without speaking a word, Rudra began to step towards her with slow, deliberate movements. Choosing caution over valor, Tisha bolted towards the door through which she had come in. Behind her, Rudra threw down the towel and sprinted behind her. Panting, she reached for more speed; if she could just get to the small back gate through which she had entered the Sheesh Mahal, she could get lost in the woods around the lake. Then, he wouldn't be able to catch her. She was smaller, slimmer, and would be able to dodge between trees he would have to go around. But as fast as she was, he still had the speed of a hawk. She saw him out of the corner of her eye, too close, and gaining ground with each long stride. He beat her by a split second, his huge body suddenly blocking her way just when she had stepped outside the door. She tried to stop, but she was already on him, and her heels weren't made for running either. She slammed into his chest, the impact knocking her breath out with a whoosh. He grunted and staggered back a few steps, his arms coming up just in time to catch her against his chest and prevent her from falling on her face.

He caught his balance and gave a muffled laugh as his arms tightened around her, holding her off the ground. "That's a pretty good hit, for a lightweight. Nice speed, too."

"I am sorry I trespassed," she said breathlessly, still finding oxygen in somewhat short supply. The tightness of his arms was interfering with her efforts to take deep breaths. She squirmed against him, then immediately stopped. The friction of his bare skin against her was too distracting, too dangerous, "I would leave soon."

"Woah! Not so soon, sweetheart. You will leave when I tell you to leave."

Wordlessly, she thought of his last words, when he had told her that he never wanted to see her again, while Rudra desperately tried to piece together his thoughts, "You could not have known that I was going to be in Sheesh Mahal, so you are definitely not here to see me," he said very softly, the velvety sound as chilling as the night air, "Care to tell me what in the name of God do you think you're doing?"

His wrists were squeezing her shoulders, bared by her sleeveless t-shirt; his skin felt hot against hers. His wide shoulders and broad chest were like a wall in front of her, and his rich, musky male scent made her nostrils flare in automatic delight. His pulse throbbed visibly in the hollow at the base of his throat, right in front of her eyes. Tisha fastened her gaze on that rhythmic movement, desperately seeking to steady herself. Swallowing a lump, she managed to say, "What are you talking about?"

He leaned closer, so close that his face was level with hers. "I'm talking about all those questions you've been asking. Di told me last week you'd been to her home."

She looked up at him. She wanted to reiterate what she suspected, but the words seem stuck in her throat. She knew he wouldn't believe her if she told him the truth. So instead she told him what was both the truth in substance and a lie in intent, murmuring, "I went there because I wanted to see you. And then we got talking."

Standing so close to her, he was acutely aware of her every movement. He shifted his hands a little and looked deep into her eyes. In the heat of the moment, her admission played like wildfire in his mind. He forgot about his mother, about Anjali, about everything else except the simmering heat between them.

"I wanted to see you too," he said softly, "I missed you."

Her breath caught. She didn't have to look up to see if he was telling the truth; she could feel the warmth in his voice and could feel it seeping right through her body. She stared helplessly at him. Color darkened his high cheekbones, and his breathing deepened. "Tisha," he murmured.

Suddenly, the tension felt like a cord between them, thrumming with awareness. She felt as if the cord were being reeled in, inexorably pulling them together. Panicked, she flattened her hands on his chest and pushed, with a total lack of results. "Rudra," she said weakly. "We can't!"

He wasn't listening. His eyes were fastened on her mouth.

"What?" he said in an absent tone as his hands tightened on her waist and pulled her against him. She moaned aloud at the feel of his strength pressed on her. He bent his head to kiss her, and she automatically lifted her mouth.

His lips brushed back and forth across her ear, then his tongue touched the lobe and began delicately tracing each curve, slowly probing each crevice, until Tisha shivered with the waves of tension shooting through her. The instant he felt her trembling response, his arm tightened, supporting her, while he deepened the kiss. His hand curved around her nape, sensually stroking it, and he began trailing scorching kisses down her neck to her shoulder. His warm breath stirred her hair and his whisper was achingly gentle as his mouth began retracing its stirring path to her ear again. "Don't be scared, I'll stop whenever you tell me to."

Imprisoned by his protective embrace, reassured by his promise, and seduced by his lips and caressing hands, Tisha clung to him, sliding slowly into a dark abyss of desire where he was deliberately sending them both. She barely realized when he had carried her to his room and lowered her on the bed.

"This is playing with fire," he said as he lowered himself next to her, on the bed, "It is not what I do very often. But tonight I am convinced that some things are worth the risk."

Before she could ask him what he meant by that, Rudra was already cradling her in his left arm. The heat was beating behind them, and with a silent moan, Tisha curled her hand behind his head and turned into his body. It was all the encouragement Rudra needed.

He did not take his hands off the bedpost on either side of her head, but he leaned forward until his mouth hovered just above hers. He intended to kiss her, she thought, but he was giving her time to protest or bolt for the door.

A wild, reckless rush of sensation swept through her. The last thing she wanted to do tonight was run from him. Quite the opposite. Everything in her yearned to drown into his embrace and allow herself to experience the mysteries of the passion that she knew she would find in his arms.

Unable to resist, she kissed his throat and then his shoulder.

He shuddered.

His response encouraged her to move her palm lower, gliding across the sleekly muscled expanse of his torso until she was stopped by the waistband of his boxers.

He made a sound that was half groan and half muffled laugh and captured her exploring hand. She closed her eyes very tightly against the bright, shivery thrills that were tripping through her. His hand left hers and she realized that he was fumbling with the opening of his boxers.

"Please no," she gasped before she could stop herself.

"'What's wrong?" He asked, bending his head to kiss her throat. "Are you all right?"

"Yes, yes, of course," She shut her eyes, too afraid to speak and break the magic that was happening between them. But all of was making her overwhelmed. Steeling her voice with a resolve she didn't quite feel, she urged, "We need to stop."

"We sure don't!"

"If you knew why I am here, you will probably ask me to get out right now."

"You are here because you wanted to see me… because you couldn't stop thinking about me… because there were so many times that you picked up your phone and almost called me up!" Rudra bit his lips to stop himself from spilling out more of his own emotions.

Tisha closed her eyes and wondered if Rudra was mocking her feelings towards him. Tears of frustration threatened to spill, but she had a far more important task at hand... a task that she was sure he would not like, "I didn't even know you were in Lucknow, remember? I came here hoping to see aunt Ambika. I read that souls tend to linger around the place they had spent most of their lives. And I was talking to people..."

Rudra held her hands, effectively stopping any further words she planned to speak. Taking few deep breaths, he tried to calm his own erratic heart. When he spoke, his voice had the poise he wanted, "I loved my mother more than anything in my life Tisha. Her life was all around di and me. My dad was rarely home because of business, but I rarely saw mom complaining to him. On the night she... died," he paused to choose the right words, "... or murdered, I remember there was a fight between my parents. Mom was accusing dad of having an affair."

"And?" Tisha gently prodded.

"And then she died!" he snapped, "Now can we bury this whole issue or you have any more questions?"

~~~

Two days later, Tisha was alone in her home, in Lucknow. She had not heard back from Rudra, but from the way he had stormed out that night, leaving her alone in Sheesh Mahal, she knew not to expect anything from him. Her mind was still reeling with the whole mystery surrounding Ambika Singh Shekhawat.

Who could have possibly been responsible for her death? Maybe her husband? No. From what she had learned from Anjali, he had been totally in love with his wife and he made up for his absence by taking them on frequent vacations. Then, was it someone from the family?

An obsession seemed to engulf Tisha as she went by her evening chores when the mailman came with letters from the past two weeks. Amidst the usual assortment of bills, magazines, and sales papers lied a gift-wrapped box. Curiously she picked it up; she hadn't ordered anything, but the weight of the box was intriguing. The flaps had been sealed with shipping tape, and her name and address were scrawled across the top. Curiously, she took it to the kitchen and kept it on the shelf. There was an envelope stuck to it, which had a folded piece of paper inside. Wondering, she unfolded it and saw the block letters.

STOP ASKING QUESTIONS ABOUT AMBIKA SINGH SHEKHAWAT IF YOU KNOW WHAT'S GOOD FOR YOU.

Not paying any heed to the note, she took out a knife from the cabinet drawer and slit the tape down the seam of the flap, and opened the two halves. After one horrified glance, she turned and vomited into the sink.

CHAPTER EIGHT

The bird wasn't just dead. It had been mutilated. It was wrapped in plastic, to keep the stench from alerting anyone before the box was opened. Tisha reacted instinctively. As soon as the violent retching had stopped, she had reached out to her phone and called Rudra. He had reached in an hour. After incessant swearing, he had been quick to get rid of the dead bird in the packet. And then he had flown her to Delhi claiming that it was not safe for her to stay in Lucknow. Rudra had even forbidden her to stay on the college campus and had brought her to his home while he excused himself to freshen up.

Sitting huddled in the spacious dining hall of Shanti Niwas, Tisha shuddered at last evening's memory. Despite the hustle-bustle going around her, her mind was busy playing the reasons behind her getting the threatening letter.

And the more she thought, the more she was convinced that it had to be an inside job. Someone from the family didn't want her to pursue Ambika's death.

Who else could possibly know of her location and her involvement with Ambika? Was it Rudra himself, or Anjali... or their aunt, Renuka? Or was someone else involved! Her mind puzzled over the bare minimal facts she had access to, and she zeroed in on her next steps.

"You have gone so pale Tisha," Anjali fussed over her health, "Did you guys fight or something?"

"No di. Everything is okay. I was wondering umm..." she looked around towards Renuka, "Can I use your washroom Renu aunty?"

"I thought you would prefer to use the one attached to Rudra's room," Renuka winked at her slyly and then sobered up, "Anyway, I think mine is the closest. You know where it is. Go ahead!"

"Thank you, Renu aunty."

Freshening up was just an excuse.

As soon as she entered, Tisha latched the door carefully. She looked around. The décor in the room was minimal. One of the walls boasted of a huge portrait of a newlywed Renuka standing with her husband and a young Rudra and Anjali. The couple looked obviously in love. Instinctively, Tisha started checking the drawers in the cabinet near the bed. She was only mildly irritated when she couldn't find anything of use. *She barely knew what she was looking for!* Briefly, she looked behind her shoulders and listened for any footsteps coming her way. Then she opened the cupboards and started looking there. One of the drawers contained a key, a silver box, and some jewelry. After sorting through the jewelry, she lifted the silver box and opened it. It contained a Mangalsutra. Oddly, she tried to recollect why it looked so familiar... then with a quick jolt it hit her.

It was Ambika's! She immediately took out her mobile and opened the pic of the sketch that Ambika had made her draw when they were looking for her wedding chain. It was almost alike... *it had to be the same one!*

She felt off-balance at the moment. The Mangalsutra! Ambika had wanted it so badly. Would she come in front of her, now that she had finally found it?

The cheerful banter in the dining hall halted when Tisha entered, the wedding chain tightly clutched in her fist. She saw Rudra sitting on one end, with a cup of coffee in his hand. Renuka was fussing over feeding him lunch.

One look at her pale face and stricken eyes and Rudra knew something was wrong. Within a minute, he was by her side. She simply stared at him, her big eyes filled with alarm.

"Are you all right Tisha?" He demanded roughly.

Tisha swallowed, words sticking in her throat. Her insides were clenching, and she turned and walked towards Renuka. Holding out her hand, she opened her fist, "I found this in your room."

The elder lady's eyes darkened with distress at the sight and her cheeks lost a shade. Renuka stared at her palm, the seconds ticking away in silence. Tisha waited for a denial, but instead, Renuka gave a curiously gentle sigh. "This is Ambika di's necklace. I thought I had lost it. Where did you find this?"

"In your drawer," she said simply, "I think you stole it."

"Why would I do that?" Renuka was genuinely surprised at the accusation, "Didi was unhappy with her marriage. I think she was considering ending her life and that is why she had given it to me during her last days. She said she wanted me to have it for Rudra's wife."

"I don't believe you," Tisha almost shrieked, "I am taking this with me. Aunt Ambika has been looking for this and she cannot find peace until she has it back."

"You care about bringing peace to her?" Renuka said sarcastically, while she snatched the chain from her, "Don't forget that you are the one who had disrupted the ritual we had organized for bringing peace to her soul."

"Enough!" Rudra interfered before the situation got out of hand, "Tisha, you need to rest. Renu aunty has been like a mother to me. It is wrong of you to accuse her just because you found my mom's chain in her drawers."

"Tisha!" Anjali spoke up, her eyes swimming with unshed tears, "how do you know so much about our mother?"

"Because she told me herself!" In the heat of the moment, Tisha screamed out the truth. She didn't care how it looked to others, but the next few minutes of stillness that followed told her how stunned everyone was. It was Rudra who dispelled the bubble of silence that had shrouded the space.

"As I said, Tisha is not well di. I am taking her to a doctor," Rudra cupped her elbow and looked sharply at her, daring her to argue.

It wasn't until they were out of the house and into the parking that Tisha shrugged his hand away, "I don't need an escort. And I don't need to see a doctor."

"Get in the car," he said, that soft, steely edge in his voice that said he'd made his decision and wasn't going to change it. "I am not taking you to a doctor. But you are for sure not safe here."

He was propelling her toward the car, and Tisha didn't waste her time arguing. She simply wanted to get away from him, and the fastest way to do that was to give in and get it over with.

He opened the car door and urged her inside with a hand on the small of her back. She sat down, sighing shakily at the relief of being off her trembling legs. He walked around and slid under the steering wheel, his hands sure and competent as he started the motor and put the transmission into gear. "Are you hungry?" he asked, that muted anger humming through his tone.

"No," she murmured, then lapsed into silence. Maintaining that silence seemed to be both the safest and easiest thing to do, so she concentrated on staring at the dark trees sliding past the car window. The car looped around the busy roads and then entered the highway. She noticed that he was taking her out of the city and at the moment she didn't care. For all the tension, she felt grateful that she didn't have to walk, else, in her present state of mind, she would have stumbled over every root and rock in her path.

The tumultuous events of the day had left Rudra more than a little shaken himself. First, there was finding that damn mangled bird in Tisha's house in Lucknow, then the frustration of trying to convince her that she could be in danger, damn it, and it would be in her own best interest if she moved away from Lucknow. She had listened to him, believed him, and accompanied him on his fight back to Delhi. Then there was the whole row about finding his mother's lost wedding chain.

He didn't care about the Mangalsutra... but he did care about Tisha. And he believed that there must be something going on for her to talk so stubbornly about it.

He'd driven them to his farmhouse. He hoped its beauty would appeal to her and they could spend some time in complete solitude, away from the tension of the past few days. His car purred and came to a stop. Without a word, he got down and opened the door for the angry little kitten that sat with a pout on her face.

"Get down Tisha," he said as softly as he could.

"No. If you want me to come with you, you will have to carry me yourself, because I am not going anywhere with you!"

Words slipped out in automation and Tisha looked up at Rudra. His eyes were full of mirth and it looked like he was controlling his urge to laugh. *Damn, she wished she hadn't said that.*

"You know I can do exactly that! Because I am a hell of a lot bigger than you and also a lot stronger than you."

"You are nothing but a bully," she unlocked the door and got down before Rudra started to get any ideas on helping her with it.

"Maybe, but a concerned one," he chuckled and followed her inside.

"This place is beautiful!" Momentarily forgetting about her company, Tisha strolled around dreamily as she took in the beauty surrounding her. It was late in the afternoon, the sun throwing long shadows when it could manage to break through the thick trees in the lawn, but for the most part, the translucent golden light was tangled in the tops of the trees, leaving the ground mysteriously shadowed. The hot, humid summer air was redolent with the pink sweetness of honeysuckle nectar, all mingled with the rich, brown odor of the earth as well as the crisp green scent of the leaves.

"This is my farmhouse. I often come here to find peace. There is a lake at the backside of the house. We can visit it later in the evening. For now, let me show you inside."

"Why didn't you bring me here before?" She turned, only to find Rudra standing right behind her, with his arms crossed against his chest, "What is it?" She murmured.

"I don't know what happened to Ma. But someone surely wants to keep matters shut. I can't imagine anything happening to you either Tisha," he walked up to the front porch and unlocked the main door, gesturing her to follow him inside, "When I was thinking of a safe place to keep you in for a couple of days, this was the first one that came to mind."

"Oh, so that's why you brought me here?" She spoke, injecting fake disappointment in her voice.

"Why, what did you think?"

"I thought you brought a lonely girl here so that you can seduce her amidst the natural beauty."

"Well, I can't say that wasn't on my mind!" he said sensuously, "But perhaps you would like to freshen up first? While you take a shower, I can see if there are some coffee and snacks in the kitchen."

An hour later, they were sitting on the sofa, talking about mundane things while sipping freshly brewed coffee. The house was quiet, the room dim, with only one lamp on. Rudra tried to ignore the fact that she was wearing just a bathrobe. When her fingers brushed against him to take his mug, he couldn't resist anymore.

A kiss had become two, then more. His hands were in her hair, and he was groaning.

"You think I am going nuts," Tisha spoke in between kisses. The temptation searing between them was like a magnet and steel, its force irresistible.

"I believe you. And that is why I got this for you," he spoke and took out the Mangalsutra from his pocket, "I know you wanted to have it."

"Rudra, Oh!!" Words failed her as Tisha took the necklace from his hand and stroked over it, "So you believe me? You don't think I need to see a doctor?"

"No," he stroked her back, making her skin tingle and her breath shorten, "I think you need a dosage of rest. That's it," he muttered, but he was rock hard.

She closed her hand around his hair, stroking him with the same slow touch he was using on her back. "I need a dosage of you."

Before she realized it, he had shrugged off his clothes. His fingers threaded their way through her robe, finding their way to her most private parts. He started touching her most intimately, setting off an aching sensation.

The sounds of the evening began penetrating her drugged senses. Wind rifled through the long curtains, whispering in the trees surrounding them; his hand stroked soothingly up and down her spine; tears of pure confusion stung her eyes, and she rubbed her cheek against his hard chest, brushing them away in what felt to Rudra like a poignantly tender caress. Drawing a shattered breath, she tried to ask him why this was happening to her.

"Why does my heart starts beating fast whenever you are around?" she whispered against his chest.

In the dim glow of the sunset, his face was hard and dark with passion, and the eyes gazing at her upturned face were blazing with it- and yet there was as much tenderness in them as there was desire. He caught her wrist and drew her hand to his chest so that she could feel its violent pounding and know that he was as wildly aroused as she, "Because our heartbeats become one."

"Why?"

"Because I love you Tisha. And I think you too feel the same way. Hell, you have no idea how I was living all these days before I met you."

"I love you too," she responded softly, her senses still drugged from their love-making. Then, she twisted against him, seeking something more, something she could not describe.

"You are ready for me, aren't you?" he said against her mouth.

"Yes!" She had no notion of what he meant by those words, but she could give no other answer other than yes to him tonight.

He rolled on top of her. Tisha didn't wait, couldn't wait. She clasped her legs around him and lifted her hips so that he slipped inside her. Pleasure seemed to spread smoothly through her body. He was slow and deep as if he wanted to savor every moment with her. She found the rhythm and joined him in it, and despite the lack of urgency, it seemed only moments before the heat and friction grew to intolerable levels. She clung to him, her nails digging into his back, small cries breaking from her throat with each move he made into her. She felt as if he went straight into the heart of her, and she climaxed on the third deep stroke. He held himself there and shuddered violently as his release took him apart.

When it was over, Rudra simply collapsed against her, his arm curved possessively against her waist. She lay quietly for a time, taking in the sensations of the moment; the weight of Rudra's body and the lingering tenderness between her thighs.

Rudra stirred eventually, raising himself on his elbows to look down at her, "Go to sleep baby."

Tisha dozed but roused a little when he carefully withdrew from her and rolled out of bed.

"Where are you going?" she murmured, reaching out to caress his back.

"To Shanti Niwas, to get an overnight bag and some important stuff like food," he replied, and the answer seemed so prosaic she chuckled.

"I'll come with you."

"Don't bother." He zipped his fly and buckled his belt. "You need to rest. Besides, I would be back in less than an hour. Before you wake up, I will be here."

After Rudra left, sleep was the last thing on her mind. Wrapping the robe to cover her modest self, Tisha strolled towards the balcony. The rain the day before had left the air fresh and sweet and she savored the beauty surrounding the house. The balcony overlooked the lake. Moonlight glinted off the surface of the water and Tisha smiled to herself, her body brimming with the spontaneous lovemaking. Her joy was also because Rudra had just handed her the most prized possession she wanted.

Stretching out her hands, she closed her eyes and out of habit called out, "Aunt Ambika!"

There was no response. Of course, she didn't expect one to be there! Hastily, she held the chain high in her hand. Light glinted off its surface.

"Hello Tisha," said a soft voice from behind her, "I never thought you would find it!"

"Aunt Ambika! Dear God!" She turned around, searching the darkness, and suddenly spot the owner of the voice, floating by the rose plant, looking even smugger than was possible. Was her subconscious playing a joke on her or was she really there! Tisha didn't care. A strange wave of delight coursed through her,

"Ohh, aunt Ambika... I have been looking everywhere for you!"

CHAPTER NINE

Renuka stopped the car a little away from the farmhouse, pulling off the road onto pasture access. She wore dark clothes and soft-soled dark shoes, for moving quietly without being seen. It was so easy to sneak up to Tisha's house in Lucknow on foot, leaving her messages, and depart undetected. Leaving the package had required more planning since it had been daylight, but Tisha had simplified things by not being at home. It had just been a matter of slipping the package into the mailbox and driving away.

She got out of the car, pistol in hand, and stepped into the dark road. There wasn't much traffic on this road even during the daytime, and if a car did come along, she would be able to both see and hear it in plenty of time to hide. In the meantime, the road was the easiest walking and left no footprints. She didn't find Rudra's car in the parking and knew without a doubt that Tisha was inside the farmhouse, alone.

"I can't believe you set me up with your son!" Tisha shrieked, "What was that about? And then to disappear on our first date! Where were you all this time? I looked everywhere for you!"

"I was visiting the world, bringing myself up to speed. So much has changed since the last time..." she gave a smile and kept her voice low, "well, since the time I was alive."

"You were visiting the world..." she repeated her words, "And what about me? You ditched me!"

"I needed you to find my chain! I did what I had to do. Besides, I don't see you complaining," Ambika spoke in an amused tone and a faint blush tinged Tisha's cheek. She changed the topic, "I found your chain in Renu aunty's cupboard... Do you remember her? Renuka Singh Shekhawat."

"Renuka? She married my brother-in-law?"

"What do you mean- married your brother-in-law?"

"I never really liked Renuka. I felt that she was too materialistic. I had made it clear that Manohar would never marry her. Had I been alive, Renuka would never have been a Shekhawat."

"Oh! In that case...", she started to say, but a hint of sound startled her, cutting her off.

"Are the doors locked?" Ambika enquired, "Someone's here."

Must be Rudra, Tisha thought and walked inside. She tiptoed to the railing to look down into the main hall. Nothing.

Then she heard a faint rasping sound, coming from downstairs, perhaps in the kitchen. The sound felt like one of the big knives was being drawn in the kitchen.

A woman's head came into view below. It was Renuka Singh Shekhawat.

Tisha jerked back, shock numbing her to her toes. She stumbled toward the bedroom door, not caring how much noise she made, and slammed the door shut. The lock turned easily. She dragged a chair over and wedged it under the door handle, but it seemed shaky and she wasn't certain it would hold against any force. *How much force could aunt exert?* She was certainly not thin, and perhaps she was stronger than she looked, and interior doors weren't equipped to withstand the kind of force exterior doors were.

"Damn it! What I am going to do now?" She swore and looked around, contemplating if she had enough time to call Rudra; and then realized that she can use help from another soul, "Aunt Ambika!"

"I am here!"

"It's Renu aunty!" Her teeth clattered as a chill swept her, "She is here, and she has got one of the kitchen knives. She is gonna kill me!"

"Don't panic Tisha!" Ambika said calmly, "Go inside the bathroom and lock the door from inside. There are tools in the bathroom. Tools that can come in real handy. All you have to do is use them. Get some towels and wrap them around your arms. Use anything you can to hinder her. Throw towels on her and try to get them around the knife so she can't use it. If that doesn't work, spray deodorant in her face."

"Okay," she whispered, unable to speak any louder, "How do you know so much?"

"I once had a scout training."

"Right!" The door handle rattled. She jumped and moved inside to stand by the bathroom door.

Something scratched the lock. Renu aunty was picking the lock. The bathroom lock wouldn't be any more substantial than the bedroom lock. Tisha ran into the bathroom and grabbed an armful of towels, as well as the can of spray deodorant. Doing as Ambika had said, she wrapped a thick towel around each arm. She knew why. She was supposed to use her wrapped arms to deflect the knife.

The door opened, shoving the chair aside. Renuka didn't say anything, just entered the room in a rush, a pistol gleaming in her hand. Tisha grabbed a thick towel and lunged at the woman, throwing all her weight at her to knock her off balance. Renuka screamed as the towel entangled her arm, but she struck anyway, and the pistol hit flat through the thick fabric. Tisha felt the kiss of it burn on her left triceps.

She didn't know how to fight. She had never fought anyone in her life. But she twisted and hammered her fist into Renuka's nose. Blood spurted, and she saw the look of shock in Renuka's infuriated eyes as if she couldn't believe anyone would dare strike her. The whole thing struck Tisha as so ridiculous that she hit her again, and again, digging her feet against the thick carpet and pushing, using all her strength and weight to push Renuka backward.

"What have I done?" she screamed, "Why do you want to kill me?"

~~~

There was a strange reddish glow in the night sky when Rudra parked his car. The glow was visible just above the trees. He stared at it, puzzled. It was a few seconds before he realized what it was, and his eyes widened with alarm. The house was on fire! And Tisha was in there, sleeping! His throat closed on a moan of terror, and he sprinted inside.

The door was unlocked, and the knob turned easily. A strange foreboding gripped him as he stepped inside the drawing hall. He stared in confusion at the strange red glow that suffused the room. The heat was more intense, and the air was acrid, burning her eyes and nose. Realization exploded in his head. Someone had poured gasoline all around the house and tossed a match to it.

And now the fire seemed to have engulfed the entire space!

He could hear some noise upstairs from his bedroom. Desperate to get Tisha away from the heat, he deliberately walked into the fire. He stopped as fits of coughing racked him. He could hear Tisha coughing and gasping, and he kept a hard grasp on her arm, forcing her towards himself.

"No," someone said hoarsely, with horror in the tone. The crackle and roar of the flames almost drowned out the words. "Rudra, what are you doing here?"

Rudra straightened slowly, automatically tucking Tisha behind him. They were caught between two dangers, the fire at the back and the pistol in the hands of the woman who had been his mother and lifelong friend.

"No," Renuka whimpered, her eyes white-edged with panic. She shook her head in denial of Rudra's presence. "I thought she was alone! I swear, Rudra, I would never have put you in danger – "

Several ugly suspicions were crowding his mind, and all of them made him sick. When he could talk, he straightened and wiped his streaming eyes with a grimy hand. "You're the one who sent that threatening note, aren't you?" he rasped, his voice so raw as to be almost unrecognizable. "And the bird... and now you set fire to a house and try to kill an innocent girl?" Rudra asked coldly, the harshness of his voice making the words even more jarring.

"I hoped she would leave," Renuka replied in a frighteningly reasonable tone. "But nothing I did made her stop, and neither did the notes. I didn't know what else to do. I couldn't let her keep asking questions, and upsetting Anjali."

Rudra gave a rasping crack of laughter. "You didn't care if di was upset," he snapped. "You were afraid she'd find out what happened to mom! You killed her!"

Rudra bellowed the accusation at her, so infuriated by the danger to Tisha and the realization that Renu aunty had killed his mother that it was all he could do to keep from leaping at her and strangling her with his bare hands. The only thing that held him back was the knowledge that, if he failed, Tisha would die.

They still stood dangerously close to the burning house, the hellish light enveloping them in a red circle beyond which nothing else existed. Renuka's face twisted with pain. "I didn't mean to!" she screamed. "I just wanted to make her understand that I loved her brother. I tried to make her see reason, but she was determined. So, I opened her medication tablets and doubled the dosage in them. I just wanted her to accept me!"

Rudra opened his mouth to contradict her. Then, to his horror, Tisha wrenched loose from his grasp and stepped out from the protection of his body. "So, you killed her," she said, her voice so rough, he could barely hear her over the roar of the hungry flames. "And then you told everyone that aunt Ambika was not happy with her marriage? You then pushed her husband to the point of suicide. There wasn't any doubt that with both dead, this matter would be buried and forgotten, was there?"

Tisha's entire body was quivering with fury, which was a mirror of his own. There wasn't much she wouldn't dare, when she had made up her mind to do it, Rudra thought proudly. She had deliberately tried to stir up a killer and bring him out into the open, even though she'd known she was putting herself at risk. Her plan had worked brilliantly, he thought viciously. *Now if he could just keep her from getting killed.*

Renuka stared at them as they struggled, Tisha trying to get away from Rudra so he wouldn't be hurt, and Rudra desperately trying to hold her close for the same reason.

"Let her go! She isn't worth it, Rudra. I'll take care of her, and everything can go on the way it was."

Suddenly, the fire started waning. The heat was gone, and fresh air rushed inside the house. Renuka stared in horror as everything started restoring itself to its original position. The chairs were straightened and pushed back under the table. The towels were wrapped neatly and placed on the bed. Her hands automatically dropped the knife and it fell a few feet away from them.

"What is going on?" She said in a bare whisper.

"Tisha," Ambika said from above them, "Take Rudra and go out from the front door. Go and call the police."

"It is payback time Renu aunty, don't you think?" Tisha said and held Rudra's hands, nudging him to follow her, "You have to trust me this one time. Please."

In less than an hour, everything was over. They went to the front lawn where his car was parked. She sat on one of the park benches while Rudra dealt with the police. Renuka was taken into custody. She looked shocked stricken and had easily confessed her crime.

"Renu aunty will serve her sentence, whatever the court decides her punishment," she said quietly to her ghost angel, "Are you okay?"

"Renuka loved Rudra and Anjali like her own children. She told me that this was the only way she could absolve her sins."

Intuitively, Tisha opened her purse and took out the Mangalsutra that had caused a ripple reaction to all of this. This was the reason why Ambika had been haunting her. Now when she gets it back... Her thoughts broke off. She realized that she wasn't ready to part away with her ghost angel. Instead, she focused her attention on the chain.

Moonlight glinted off its beads and it shimmered. It looked so stunning that Tisha had a sudden strong urge to put it on. But instead, she looked up at Ambika, who was sitting beside her, watching her silently.

"Here you are. It's yours." Automatically she tried to put it around her neck. But her hands sunk straight through her. She tried again and again and failed each time.

"It's yours! You should be wearing it!"

"I wish I could touch it!" Ambika's voice rose in sudden tension and then she moved away, her eyes fixed on the paving slabs of the courtyard. "I cannot take it Tisha. It belongs to Rudra's wife now."

Before Tisha could make sense of the mystical statement, she saw Rudra coming towards her. His eyes were cast downward, and he looked exhausted as he took his seat next to her on the park bench.

"Are you okay?" He tried to smile despite the weariness weighing him down.

"I'm fine, just tired."

He nodded, then simply put his arms around her and folded her against him, sighing deeply as he absorbed her nearness. The events of the evening were still catching up with him; part of him felt numb, while another part was still aching with almost inexpressible grief. He tilted her head up with his fingers, dark eyes boring into hers. "The doctor couldn't explain Renu aunty's condition. They think that the shock has paralyzed her."

"But, what do you think?"

He kissed her instead, the pressure of his mouth warm and hard. "How do you think mom would have felt, had she been here?" He whispered hoarsely.

Numbly, Tisha looked at Ambika, who nodded back to her, "Tell my son that I am glad I got this chance to come and meet you both. Tell him that I never blamed him for anything, and I am proud of the person he has become."

"I think Aunt Ambika would have been very proud of you Rudra," a film of tears pooled in her eyes, "If she were here, she would have told you how much she loves you."

"What happens now?" She asked looking at Ambika, through Rudra.

"It is time for me to go now."

For a moment, Tisha didn't move. She had been chasing it, hunting it, and wishing for it, but now she wanted this time to stand still. She tightly held on to Rudra and closed her eyes.

When she opened them, Ambika was gone, *forever*!

"No!" she let out a whimper, "She is gone Rudra. She didn't even take this. What am I supposed to do with her Mangalsutra?"

"I think this chain has already found its new owner," he said metaphorically, pressing his lips to her temple, "Tisha, would you marry me?"

CPSIA information can be obtained
at www.ICGtesting.com
Printed in the USA
LVHW011053310322
714806LV00004B/781